T0209639

SEEING THINGS IN
BLACK AND WHITE

ANTOINE K. STROMAN

authorHOUSE

AuthorHouse™
1663 Liberty Drive
Bloomington, IN 47403
www.authorhouse.com
Phone: 1 (800) 839-8640

Published by AuthorHouse 05/06/2020

ISBN: 978-1-7283-6108-6 (sc)
ISBN: 978-1-7283-6107-9 (e)

I grew up in a predominantly black neighborhood, and didn't understand the power of being black until I was placed in an environment where black wasn't predominant. It was then that I realized just how beautiful black truly was...

–Antoine K. Stroman

This book was written between August 2011 and October 2019.

"America wants to go back to a time where TV was in black and white, and so was everything else..."

–Gil Scott Heron

CONTENTS

PART 1

PART 2

▼

Chapter 1

All Was Created Equal?

· · · · · · ·

Growing up in the inner-city isn't always the greatest experience, but at the same time, it's far from the worst. I used to envy the white folks who grew up in suburbia with their harmless dogs, front lawns, nice houses and quietness in contrast to the commotion and noise down here where I grew up. Those kids were educated, I learned eventually, and always wondered why it seemed we could not get ahead. My mother and father sent me to school every day and emphatically told me, "If you want to change things, you have to be the one to do it, and the only way to do it, is by getting educated." I went to school everyday with that in mind, that and what my friends and I were going to get into. We worked hard in school, turning the F-environment that we lived and went in, into A+ 's in the classroom. However, we also played hard; I mean we were kids, what do you really expect? We went outside every single day and played hard until we smelled like "outside", as my mom used to put it. I can remember playing basketball until my clothes were so sweat drenched, that it looked like I ran through a water plug and football, laying out for passes on the concrete, shattering people's windows in the process. I also remember how adamant we were about becoming football and basketball stars. Michael Jordan, Deion Sanders, and Randall Cunningham were just a few of the guys that we admired. We believed that because of the situations that we lived in, (the ghetto), that that was the gateway to a "the life", never mind that we were A+ students. Nobody ever told us or even gave us a chance to be a Martin Luther King. Instead they made

Dr. King seem like this untouchable black being, placing him on this pedestal, as if there will never be another black like him, like nobody should even aspire to be like him or something. I guess if that's their reaction, then I am quite certain that they do not want another Malcolm X. I remember seeing the sign in my elementary school, "Knowledge is Power!" painted in big red letters on the stairway. I thought, "that has to be the cheesiest thing that I have ever heard. If they want us to stay in school, why don't they simply say it." You know I never understood why they used to just beat around the bush in want to say anything because they did not want to 1) put thoughts in our heads when we are at an age where everything influenced us, and 2) they probably did not want to say, "We know your thinking about having sex, and we don't want you to feel awkward." Who knows though, because I don't. When I got into high school, I thought that I had things figured out, I knew that in the inner-city schools they won't be straightforward with me about anything, and the best they can do to encourage me was to place signs around the classroom that read phrases like, "You can do it!" or "Books are the Bomb!" I also understood that all I was thought to be able to accomplish being a kid from the inner-city was to rap or play ball. So, I decided I had no choice other than to settle for some sort of career, I mean blacks like Dr. King were rendered untouchable by my society, and I had no idea of the power that was in knowledge. That all changed one day in January of my senior year.

On the coldest day of the year, you would've thought that the rapture had taken place as school was seemingly empty. My history teacher, Mr. Coles, was a rather interesting fellow. He was somewhat of a square, clean cut, and seemingly a bit docile. He did almost everything by the book; all of his lessons were concrete, and left little to no room for political incorrectness. Well, on this particular day, Mr. Coles had apparently eaten his Wheaties as he decided to veer away from our topic, "Reaganomics", and teach us about the dueling philosophies of Booker T Washington and WEB Dubois: two prominent black figures that I had heard of, but never actually been taught about. Standing before an almost empty classroom, he began by asking us to move our seats up, so that he didn't have project his voice. He started by explaining the philosophy of the "Talented Tenth", which was met by just about every hand in the desolate classroom. "How?" "That's ridiculous!", "So I'm a follower if I'm not apart of that ten percent?"

I sat quietly as I watched my peers totally rip Mr. Coles with questions. I pondered the validly of this philosophy, as exclusive as it may come off, was he right? I mean, maybe there would never be another Dr. King, or, perhaps it just wasn't meant for us to proceed him. I suddenly snapped back into reality when Mr. Coles had received a call on the classroom phone. Signaling at me, he said, "You're wanted in the counselor's office." So, I grabbed my backpack, and headed downstairs to see what my counselor wanted. As I walked down the long hallway, I was met with this strange mix of emotions; an optimistic pessimism, to some extent. I reflected very heavily on the class discussion, as I walked into the counselor's office to, surprisingly, all smiles. Each of the counselors were seated at their respective desks and made it a point to be incredibly cordial to me. I mean, unusually cordial. Walking past one of the female counselors, I was actually greeted with a hug. Her arms were stretched out as she sported a mystic look in her eyes, combined with a smile of approval. It almost seemed as if she had been greeting the President during one of those political campaigns, where they excite people to the point of hero worship. I finally reached my guidance counselor, Mr. Tomas. I always thought it was odd that he wanted us to call him Mr. THOMAS, despite his Spanish heritage. I wonder if he thought we wouldn't be able to pronounce it, or something. Mr. Tomas was a tall, thin man, who was incredibly patriotic. He had the American flag plastered above his college Alma Mater's flag, The University of Alabama, along with this copy of the U.S. constitution. "Hey you!" He shouted upon seeing me. I always found it funny that he didn't really know my name. "Hey Mr. Tomas. What's up?" I responded quizzically. "Have a seat son. You are the recipient of a high honor. It's called the W.E.B Dubois scholarship. You are the first ever recipient from our school... And we are so proud to be able to boast having you! You are truly representative of what our school is all about, sending kids to college! Now, aside from the scholarship money you'll receive, there are a lot of people that are going to want to speak to you, namely about our school. So, we want to make sure you're able to knock every question out of the park. Here is a list of frequently asked questions and

▼

Chapter 2

The Freshmen 15

· · · · · · ·

I watched the squirrels prance across the lawn as I headed to class on the first day. It was a warm, breezeless late August morning and students, mostly freshman, seemed to fill the campus. As I approached the stairway to the academic building, smiling at my freshman colleagues, who were smiling back at me, I was met with this strange combination of emotions; optimism and pessimism, tranquility and anxiety. I grabbed my roster, which was printed on a huge sheet of white paper, and actively searched for my first class. Once I had found the classroom, I stealthily moved through the hallways and found a seat in the empty lecture hall. I was early, so I sat for a moment to take it all in. I couldn't believe I was sitting in a classroom that big... I mean, it looked like a miniature opera house. I realized I had gotten to class about a half hour early, so I thought I'd just sit and soak it all in; this was college, it was my future. As I sat and pondered, a young lady came and sat two seats away from me. She had blonde hair, wintry blue eyes and was sporting a denim jean skirt/shirt set. "Hi" she said with a great sense of excitement. "Hey", I replied apathetically. "This is exciting", she went on. "I've never felt so nervous. I mean, my first college class... this is great. After my parents dropped me off for the freshman orientation, I've been giddy." I thought she was done, but she continued. "Wow, my first English class. I love English... Shakespeare, Chaucer, Moser, Elliot and all of the greats. I remember in 11th grade, we read Othello and I was just like... ahhhhh... it was awesome.. The racial dichotomy presented was simply astounding... What's your favorite text to read?" I had began tuning her out, but her question brought me back into the moment. I honestly didn't want to tell her that my favorite text was, well, nothing. I wasn't quite introduced to some of the authors she was naming; I mean, I didn't even know who Chaucer or Moser we're, and Othello, I had heard of it, but I knew nothing of it. I tried to just laugh it off and avoid the question, but she was persistent. "Well, do you like Shakespeare? Everyone likes Shakespeare. Shakespeare is awesome. I remember we read the story The Tempest. It was really cool. Have you read that story?" Trying to avoid the conversation, I laughed it off and nervously slipped to the restroom.

Looking in the mirror, I thought, "I don't belong here. These kids are so much more prepared than I am, so much smarter." I went back into the room with my walkman on, to ensure that I wouldn't have to make conversation with anyone. The room began to fill and it seemed as if I was being suffocated, closed in by my peers, and strangled by thoughts of being a ghetto kid outside of his element. I used to be a big fish in a small pond... No... I was a killer whale in kiddie swimming pool. Now, I felt as if I was reduced to being a goldfish in the Pacific Ocean. Then, the professor walked in. He was a short man, with glasses, wearing a blazer, a white shirt and bow-tie, sporting a very smooth, James Bond-Like comb over hairstyle. He immediately began laying out his expectations which included a syllabus the size of the bible. After he laid out his expectations, which were lofty by my standards, he immediately started teaching. I had gotten lost; lost in anxiety as the teacher's voice began to fade and the sounds of the almost 300 pencils became deafening. I was stoked when class was over, feeling as if I needed to exhale, as fear, and anxiety were quite literally suffocating me. Upon coming to this revelation, I grew more nervous as the semester would progress. Thoughts would flow rapidly through my mind, as I sat nervously in class: "I don't belong here" or "These kids are so much smarter than I am." As a youngster I thought that all education was created equally, but college taught me otherwise. As a matter of fact, it taught me that social class is almost a direct correlation to that of the quality of education, it seems. And it seemed that compared to my colleagues, social class was the class that I had been failing miserably in. For my first group project in college, myself and another brother were randomly placed in a group with some of our white counterparts. My group mates all seemed to blend, while I honestly did not feel I fit in much, namely because of paranoia regarding social class. I felt as if I was intellectually inferior to my classmates and refused to really open up because of it. At one point, my black colleague, Roy, said to me "Hey, you seem so tense, what's the problem?" "I'm good, my man" I chuckled. "Are you sure? I mean, we can rap after this." I shook my head and agreement, and suddenly I felt a sense of peace fall over. I finally felt that I could get this burden off of my chest, and to someone who could actually relate to me. Interestingly, when we spoke this brother simply told me, "Hey don't worry about it", seemingly dismissing my feelings of doubt. He would add, "We all learn the same things don't we? We all take social studies, math, english and all of the other jargon, so what's the fuss?" He added, "I mean, where I'm from they teach us some pretty irrelevant things, so your situation can't be any worse." He added as he patted me on the back. "I guess you're right..." I said with a sigh. "I just don't feel I fit in man. I mean, it's there's this big party on the OUTSIDE, and I'm just stuck here, on the INSIDE." I said. "Look man, just take my word for it, I grew up around white folks... I'm a suburban kid born and bred, and I'm having a blast. What could be so different about you?"

I thought about that for a second. What could be so different about me? Why was it that this suburban kid, who was black, could fit in with white kids, while I sat in paranoia? I thought a it more as I plopped down on the bed in my dorm. I had no concept of race, or at least the concept of race I did have was predicated upon what my grandma used to tell me about what whites did to them down in the south. I didn't see a whole lot of white folks, outside of my teachers, and they often aggrandized themselves as if they were doing us a favor by dealing with us or something. While my perspective on race was certainly skewed, somehow, I had intertwined social class into the mix. More often than not, when I thought about the upper class, the higher ups in society, I thought about whites. Class, didn't necessarily have a occupation to me, it had a color. When I turned on the television and saw Congress, I saw a whole lot of white. When I would see Presidents portrayed on television, I saw white. Then, I would look around my neighborhood, at all of the working class folks, the poverty, and namely the people who looked like me, I would see black. It was almost as if white existed in a realm far, far away from me, while black was my reality.

For the next couple of days I once again stayed to myself, which wasn't quite unusual at that time, when another shocking revelation would come. Coming from a lower working class family, it is quite easy to see when things are a "step up" from normalcy, but it doesn't seem like those that truly live such a life really realize it. I had never seen so many people who take so much for granted in my entire life. It seems that there is often a sense of entitlement, like these privileges were actually rights. Many nights I left shaking my head thinking, "they just don't know how easy they have it!" It was at that point that I realized that I had something special, something unique, something that gave me an edge. I had a disadvantage! Who would've known that being relatively under educated, would actually come in handy? I once heard that a disadvantage is an advantage. Think about it; a person with a disadvantage is a person, that has nothing to lose, a person who understands what it's like to be at the bottom in some way, shape or form. Usually, this is a motivational factor to succeed, I mean after all you have nowhere else to go except for up.

From then on I embraced this disadvantage, I'd use this disadvantage... to my advantage! I began to walk with a swagger, an attitude that boisterously proclaimed, "This cat has nothing to lose!" I noticed that the loss of my timidity meant the loss of discomfort; I made a lot more friends, namely friends that didn't look like me in terms of race. My change in attitude also saw a change in terms of my grades. Due to my attitude shifting from feeling like I did not belong, to undertaking a sense of entitlement, my grades looked far better than those from when I began. I also assembled a list, something to keep me focused and to eventually pass down to those who came up like I did. I called it, "The Freshman 15". It goes as follows:

1. Preparation is key. Be prepared for everything.
2. Be self conscious... be very self conscious. You are a representation of where you come from.

3. Business before pleasure. After your classes end, go do homework, you'll appreciate it when its time to go to bed.
4. READ
5. READ some more.
6. READ even more.
7. Did, I mention read?
8. Make your mind your business and your business your mind.
9. Be on time. Period.
10. Discipline is everything. Motivation runs out.
11. Responsibility never takes a day off.
12. Read.
13. Be not intimidated by your colleagues.
14. Read
15. After you've accomplished these... have fun.

Chapter 3

The Hustler's Mente

• • • • • • •

College would be a blur and before I knew it, I was a senior preparing to graduate. Graduation was an exciting time for me; as not a lot of brothers who came from where I came from had the opportunity to experience it. It didn't hit me as to how important this event was until I received my cap and gown. I remember feeling the strangest blend of excitement and anxiety; optimism and pessimism, joy and sadness. Though I was earning my degree, which was the source of these positive emotions, I couldn't shake the thoughts of being unsuccessful. I mean, a degree is cool, but it's only half of the story. As the days drew near, this premonition would increase. The horror stories I had heard of college grads "success" stories not finding good jobs, was playing over in my mind like a song on repeat. I didn't want to be the person with a degree and a million dollar smile with nothing to show for either one. I immediately began applying for employment opportunities, with hopes that I could be a success story, but these days it's not necessarily what you know, but who you know. Being from the ghetto, I don't know too many higher ups, business folk etc. I just wanted to break the mold, be different, make things better for my children and their children. I had visions of getting into local politics. Yeah, not one of those folks who abuse good morals and good people, but the real type. The type of person who that makes honesty numero uno! I grew up with a sense of integrity, therefore I felt it was my duty to be a compliment to my race and maintain it.

see it from the perspective of the "here and now" and never really think about the fact that they too have a story, and it doesn't always have anything to do with drugs. Thoughts about this guy's situation stayed plastered across my mind as we arrived at Grand Central Station. We were back in New York, where the only thing higher than the prices is the population. As we walked through Times Square, I saw an influx of homeless individuals, all who seemed to be staring at me as if they knew I had the conversation earlier with the guy on the train. It was as if they were all linked: all homeless and, in a place like New York City, nameless. They were nameless in a place where the darkness and lifelessness is seemingly offset by the bright lights and lively vibes of Times Square. We maneuvered our way through the congestion of midtown Manhattan as we made our way to the train. We got a bit tangled up and ended up on Park Avenue near a high-end district. There weren't many people who looked like us there, needless to say. It was early in the afternoon, so herds of people were out on the streets shopping, going for walks, etc. Rolling our suitcases along, we asked a few people for directions on how to catch the train. Many of them looked at us like we had seven heads, before giving us a template answer on how they didn't know. We walked into a very ritzy store to get directions, and were greeted with looks from shoppers. We heard "Front to manager, front to manager" over the PA system as the classical music commenced in the background. We searched for someone to help us and ended up being greeted by a tall, thin man wearing an immaculate suit. He had a tight British accent, and asked us rather pretentiously, "You two must have wandered to the wrong side of town. How can I help you?" "We actually did wander to the wrong side of town, and we just wanted help getting back to the Metro" I replied with a bit of disgust. Mildly sucking his teeth, he replied beneath his breath, "I didn't think you monkeys wanted anything, anyways..." At that, my brother Cecil responded hastily, "What!!!" He grabbed the man's well-fitted suit, gripping him up. Before I could respond, the security had already drawn tasers on us, as I attempted to pull my brother away. I grabbed my brother, aggressively just before the guards could catch him. As I pulled him away from the situation, another set of guards grabbed us and tossed us out of the store like Jazz would be tossed out by Uncle

Seeing Things In Black and White

Phil on Fresh Prince. About a second after being hurled face first into the ground, I realized we didn't have our bags.... that is until I heard a crash just one second later. They had tossed out our precious cargo, our meal ticket, our very purpose for being in this city. I wiped a bit of gravel off of my face as we got up to look into our bags, hoping that the impact didn't do as much damage as it had sounded. We opened our bags only to find that the products had been destroyed. My brother was furious, and while I was furious, I thought, "at least I have an excuse to not do this anymore." I was at a place where I was no longer interested in making a sum, I was interested in making a difference.

▼

Chapter 5

"Excess Granted"

• • • • • • •

We left New York City rather unceremoniously, and I felt the strangest blend of emotions; optimism and pessimism, anxiety and tranquility. Why I actually felt optimistic, despite losing what could have earned me a new laptop, new kicks, etc., I'm not 100 % sure. It may have had something to do with the fact that I no longer had an excuse to do something that I really didn't want to do in the first place. On the way home I couldn't help but think about the guy's story from the train. Now that I think of it, maybe that's the reason why I felt so relived. I mean, consider my position; if things had gone to plan, I would be on my way home considering futile ways to spend my money, while this dude and others, are struggling to get to where I am just to take care of basic necessities. Completely turned off by that, on top of the racial, classist issues we'd encountered, and the fact that I personally wasn't where I wanted to be, I sprinted off the train once we made it home. My brother wanted to go out and sulk in our sorrows, but I needed to seek solace in solitude. I needed a plan; I needed to get to where I wanted to be.

On my way home, I ran into a heard of the homeless on the city's main strip, some asking for money, some weren't. There was one dude who was homeless, but based on his disposition, you wouldn't think so as he was telling jokes to all that walked by him. I thought his jokes were actually pretty funny and something inside propelled me to give him some money. I didn't have much to give him, but I had a home to go to, with food in it, so it was the least I could do. Instead of simply giving him money and walking away, I wanted to know a little bit about him, I wanted to hear his story. "Sir, how..." Before I could complete my thought he interrupted calmly, "how did I get here?" I shook my head in affirmation as he continued, "Well, this happened to me right after the Clinton Administration. I was working in a business down here." He pointed to the tallest building in the city, the Aspro building. "I had eventually gotten an office, after having been there for 20 years, and I was living comfortably. Then, things started to change. I noticed that they began to change their policies for certain things, me not having a college education, was one of the first to go. I asked the boss why I was being relieved so quickly, considering I had been with the company for over two decades. His response was something to the effect of 'well, we want to take this company in the right direction, so we want to add people with better education.' Education wasn't played up well when I was growing up. In the black community you could go to college, and if you did you represented a very small percentage of blacks, so the common thread was for you to just get a job, and be content with staying there. Try to move around if you can, but be grateful that you can eat. Well, after I lost my job, I had to relinquish my apartment, my car, everything. I couldn't maintain. Before I knew it, I was out here. The people at McDonalds wouldn't even hire me because they see me walking the streets and believe that I'm some drunk, or some drug addict because I don't have a home." I was yet again astonished. After exchanging sentiments I wished him good luck as we parted ways. As I walked away from him, I gazed upon the slew of bodies, realizing that each had their own story for how they had been introduced to the streets. I didn't have much money, but I tried to drop in at least a dollar to each person I had seen, just because I felt compelled to do so. What's interesting is that a strange sense of satisfaction came over me, almost instantly appeasing the anger I had felt from the events of the weekend.

For the remainder of the week, I had begun seeking ways to give to others, because for some odd reason, that brought me satisfaction. Seeing the smiles on their faces, the elation radiating from their hearts actually made me fell pretty good about myself. I had always dreamed of being a politician for the sake of making conditions better for people, and here I as doing it! I can remember being out one day in February

Antoine K. Stroman

"REVITALIZE OUR NEIGHBORHOOD!!!! COME TO THE COMMUNITY CENTER ON SOUTH BUSH STREET TO FIND OUT HOW!!!!"

I showed my brother, and tilting his head slightly to the right, he responded, "It's straight to the point … still kind of sounds like something out of a kid's show, but I get it. One question though, 'What's going to get people to come out?'" I thought about that, as my initial thought was, "The meeting is the draw, ain't it?" He suggested a small change, and since he "knows people", according to him at least, I listened and added it in. We really blitzed the area, posting signs on every storefront, bando, light pole, and mailbox we could find.

On the day of the meeting, I felt the strangest blend of emotions; an anxiety that this wouldn't resonate, but a tranquility that at least I was doing it. We set the meeting time for 5PM, and by 5:15 we had close to a full house. Maybe my pessimism was all for naught, maybe we were going to do this thing, maybe my dreams were going to come true! Well, it initially seemed that way.

I began speaking to the people about the history of our area, how jobs had become scarce and there were no black owned businesses in our area. I counted about 3 out of the 30 people actually listening, and I even spotted my brother in the back true to talk to girls. I spoke for 5 long minutes, which seems like 5 hours when no one is listening, and finally released everyone to eat. The tide of the room quickly shifted as people went from lethargic to livewires once the food was served. "I sat here and poured out my passion, and all they remember is the food", I thought. A sense of sadness quickly came over me. My brother smiled jovially, and gave me the thumbs up because that was the "draw" that he had suggested, food. He came over to where I was standing, placed his arm on my shoulder and said, "I'm not sure anybody cared about what you said, but you fed the people." He gazed out at the lively crowd, who were conversing over nice hot food and continued, "You gave them what they needed … it just may not have been what you thought it was. Cheer up bro."

As we were cleaning up, and bidding people farewell, I was enamored at how many people actually felt I had done a great job, but I was still a bit down. The owner of the community center actually came up to me and offered me the center's card. "We always try to hire people from the community, but nobody seems to come to us. We'd like to have somebody like here, if you're ever interested." Considering that I was pretty low on the money I had made working with my brother, and I'd pretty much been giving it all away, I definitely planned on calling back.

Once we had wrapped up cleaning, my brother and I headed home. I felt like I had failed, despite what my brother and the woman from the community center said, so I tuned out my brother's vain conversation about the girls. I was brought back into reality when we walked past one of those storefront churches. I slowed down as we approached it, as it had a banner that read, "Now faith is the substance of things hoped for, the evidence of things unseen..."

▼

Chapter 7

"Sub – Conscious"

· · · · · · ·

I thought a lot about the banner and this "faith", so I told myself that I'd go to my old church that Sunday. I had stopped going just before I left for college because I honestly wasn't feeling compelled to stay. It seemed like I was going to a concert every week instead of a house of worship; a place where people would go show off their talents, or the latest threads and listened to a man woo them with incoherent screams and shouts. I also hated feeling judged. Every Sunday, I would watch people stare down those that may not have been dressed "up to par", or simply wearing jeans. My aunt didn't believe you needed to dress up to go to church. She always said, "God accepts us for who we are, so we should always come as such." The Pastor, Pastor Martel, seemed more concerned with what things looked like, then what was actually happening in the congregation. He was a tall, slender man, who spoke with a very deep, commanding voice, and he was always smiling.

I ended up going to the service that weekend and was met with an altogether different feeling when I walked in. The first thing I noticed was that Pastor Martel was gone, and in his place, was a short, rotund man that I had heard being referred to as Pastor "Q". I caught the tail end of his message, but the last line spoke specifically to me:

"Sometimes in life you'll be alone… And you just have to be okay with that. Everybody can't handle your struggle. Your struggle is designed just for you, because your prize for overcoming is designed just for you. As long as you stay within the will of God, you'll be fine."

This particularly interested me, because of what had just transpired at the community meeting. I mean, it is always nerve racking going into anything solo, however, those words were both nerve racking, and encouraging at same time. It was almost as if he was delivering a message to me directly.

I attempted to make an escape after church, knowing that many of the old church ladies that knew me from childhood would try to talk to me. Before I could slide out of the main chapel, one of the women grabbed me by the arm with a firm, yet comforting grasp, "Hey son!" she said with a great sense of joy. "Mrs. Cleaver?" I said quizzically as I turned to see who was speaking to me. "I knew that was you. Oh, it's ben so long. And look at you... you're so handsome." I blushed a bit, and smiled, "Thanks, Mrs. Cleaver." She grabbed me again by the arm, as if she didn't want me to leave and turned into the mass of people and yelled out, "Lee, come over here. Look what the wind blew in!" She turned back to smiling from ear to ear, when a tall thin, well-dressed man walked up, "Ohhh! Look who it is! I haven't seen you in eons young fella!" It was Mr. Cleaver, her husband. The Cleavers were close friends with my mom, who used to bring me to church, and invite us to dinner every Sunday afterward. "You look great young man, what you up to these days?" I was a tad bit embarrassed as to having not been up to anything, so I simply replied with a shrug accompanied which was accompanied by an indifferent smirk. "I'm really not doing too much", I added. Mr. Cleaver looked at me with a sinister looking grin saying, "Is that right? Well, we still run the community center down on 7th, if you'd like to come down, we do have money in our budget for another person." I tilted my head to the side and looked at him quizzically, unsure of how to respond to the proposition. Just before I could utter a word, Mrs. Cleaver, looking at Mr. Cleaver, added, "Way to put the boy on the spot Harry!" She rolled her eyes at him and continued, "But, he's right, we do have an opening for at least one more staff, and we would love to have you on staff." She began gazing distantly as she rambled on, "Man, we loved your mother. Such a strong woman... A woman with standards! She gave her life to this community... her time, her energy, her money... everything. Most importantly, she was a dear friend of ours." She seemingly snapped back into reality when she seconded Mr.

Chapter 8

"Miss" Education

· · · · · · ·

I left the building absolutely furious after the meeting ... I was pissed, to say the very least. I kept my cool, however, as I slowly walked down the long steps that led to the main street. I can remember turning my right and in the most polarizing moment of my life, seeing the most gorgeous pair of legs that I had ever seen. They were buttery brown, well lubricated and not a hair in sight. I followed those legs all the way to the summit and saw one of the most beautiful faces I had ever seen. Sporting a dark grey skirt suit with a black shirt, I thought I was in love. I had no luck with women up to that point, but something drew me to her. "Who are you kidding, that woman is on another level of beauty..." I said to myself. I'm surprised that she hadn't noticed me staring at her, for what was probably about 3 seconds, but seemed like an eternity. It didn't matter though, her beauty was an escape from the reality of what had just transpired. I fought with myself for a second, like a schizophrenic trying to make sense of life. I had nothing to lose, I had already felt dejected, so I gassed myself up to say something and just as I began to speak she looked at me and said, "They are crazy aren't they?" I sighed with relief that I didn't have to initiate conversation with this beauty and replied "tell me about it." "I used to work here, I actually just quit. Too political and it seems like they actually don't care about kids, just statistics." I thought I was in love. Who would've thought I'd meet a gorgeous sister, who shares my thoughts and feelings on the things that matter. I randomly blurted out, "I'm actually headed to grab something to eat, would you like to join me really quick?", as I quietly placed my hands behind my back, to cross my fingers, while praying in my mind. "Absolutely, that'd be cool," she answered warmly. Elated inside, I led her to this spot a couple of blocks away.

At lunch we shared our thoughts, as my adoration for this woman only increased. "It's a numbers game. It's all a numbers game. You see, at the end of the year, the state only cares about the numbers. There are two numbers in particular, though; the test scores and the budget. They look at the test scores based upon the state standard, and if schools don't meet the state standards, that are made up by PEOPLE by the way, they start looking at you funny. Then, after a while, the money will start to diminish and then closure will come. The crazy thing is that schools in the inner – city are automatically on the hot seat. They are always the first to take the hit. Isn't that something? They don't give them updated books, and take forever to modernize technology, so our kids are short changed. The terrible part is that these minority communities are hit the hardest because they make up a great percentage of this population, and kids often feel like they are being given up on. They often become hopeless, and resort violence, drug use and distribution, or just end up on the low end. It's all just a vicious cycle.... And another thing, I hate that they are beginning to put more money into the penitentiary than into the school systems these days."

I hung onto her every word, and not just because I was infatuated with her beauty. Looking at her, I saw myself as an Eldridge Cleaver type of figure, and she being my Kathleen. We would work together to conquer this issue. As she stepped away from me to answer a phone call, I daydreamed about marrying her. Yeah, I was doing the daydreaming! When she returned, I planned on asking her out on a date to get things "moving." As soon as she returned, I leaped over my fear and simply asked her if she'd like to hang out sometime. She replied, "Sure!" Completely forgetting about what happened earlier at the district building, I was absolutely elated. We set up our time and parted ways. I was excited, so much so, that for the next couple of days, I floated through my work at the community center. Mr. and Mrs. Cleaver were like, "Are you okay? I mean, you've seemed so mechanical." I'd reply, "I am mighty fine", with a smile that'd make the Kool Aid man jealous. Finally, date night had

▼

Chapter 9

Politics As Usual

· · · · · · ·

I woke up feeling a little bit better, which was a plus, and headed off to work. I received a facebook friend request from Ryan, her boyfriend. I accepted despite feeling pretty awkward about it, and wrote a friendly "how's it going?" on his wall. I really didn't want him to respond, but he did. He asked me in a message if he and I could meet, after his girl told him about my goals to improve education in the inner city. I agreed and we met up for lunch later on that day a few blocks away from my job. "Thanks for meeting up with me" he said. "I feel that a guy with your type of zeal and my insider information, we really can make a change." I shook my head slowly, as he continued, "I'm running for mayor and I feel that you'd be someone that I'd like to keep close by, as it pertains to the bettering of the community. You've got some pretty fresh ideas, and I feel you'd be a good asset. The community, the city needs people like you, folks that can relate to what they are going through. As I told you yesterday, I had that issue when I was working in the inner – city schools. So, would you mind considering it?" I wanted stay stone cold emotionally, but I couldn't. I was intrigued as I felt that my deferred dream of getting into politics was now all of a sudden revitalized. I told him I'd think about to attain a bit of mystique, but in all honesty, I was sold. I contacted him later that evening telling him that I was down. He was elated and it felt pretty good, although I did have some reservations. The campaign was to begin in a few months and I was pretty stoked, so I began working on ideas. I'd stand in the mirror like a kid before a recital and pretend that I was being called upon to drop a few words. I even went as far as to buying a pair of black sunglasses reminiscent of Fred Hampton, whose speeches inspired me. As the time to campaign grew nearer, at least the action, and the meetings got lengthier, I tried to assert myself more, but only found myself muzzled by the higher – ups. It felt like it was their campaign and I was just a body. I was the only black man on the job and the fact that I felt like they didn't really listen to me, only added to me feeling that there were might have been racial undertones at work. However, I just stayed cool, and refuted the idea of jumping to that conclusion. Ryan, noticing that I was sad, came over to me and asked if I was okay. I replied, "I'm good, but to be honest I feel like I'm not being listened to." "I apologize if it comes off that way, everyone is just really uptight these days you know. We're just trying to get the job done," he added. I slightly shrugged my shoulders, and left the room.

The next day I was greeted with a smile as I headed into the meeting, and I was painfully curious as to why. I finally grabbed one of the guys and asked what was going on, and with a smile he said, "It's time for the first major speech, everyone gets excited around this time." Again, I shrugged my shoulders and went on about my business. In the meeting, Ryan pointed me out and said, "Let's see what you know, bro." Confused, I asked him exactly what he meant with such a statement. "It's time for you to implement your ideas, so we can win this race" he explained. I thought, "Wow, they are finally listening! I've got their attention." I began by asking them how they felt about certain issues, I mean it's a group effort isn't it? They replied, in a rather smug manner, "Whatever you feel, we feel." "Really?" I replied in an uncertain manner. "Yes, really" they replied back seemingly in unison. I stood there as the silence in the room screamed at me, until Ryan stood up and pulled me to the side. "Listen, I told you I'd bring you here for your ideas, and that's what I want right now. I want your ideas. You asked for our attention, now you've got it. I see something in you and it needs to come out, it's now or never. We've got to have you here to pull out this victory." All of a sudden, I felt a sense of power. You know, that control when a singer steps on stage and everyone gets quiet. That type of control, when the audience waits with anticipation for the performer to do something great. That feeling that they will go where you will take them, whether you take them to the moon, Tokyo, or just up the street. I stood back in front of my seat and pointing to each individual, asked them what changes they wanted to see. Each either shrugged their shoulders, or gave some ludicrous answer plagued by stammering, "um's" and stuttering. It then became clear as the chorus of Stevie Wonder's song, "Big Brother", came to my mind. These men weren't really concerned with the inner city or me, for that matter, they wanted a vote; they wanted power. It all made sense as to why they didn't seem to take me seriously, until now that is, until they needed me. I thought it was sad and pathetic as I went on to convey my thoughts and ideas to a bunch of guys that couldn't care less. I had no issue that they didn't relate, nobody relates to everyone, but I had a serious issue with the fact that they didn't care to understand. They all gave me positive feedback and assured me that my ideas would help them pull out the win. I felt like a serious sellout, like I was letting the robber into the house. However, in all of this, I came to a very important conclusion, I had the power in this equation.

▼

Chapter 10

Setting The Record Straight

· · · · · · ·

I just so happened to flip past professional wrestling the following evening and was fascinated with one of the fellows I saw. What intrigued me about this gentleman was the fact that he said what he felt. Now, don't get me wrong, I understand that wrestling is scripted, but I felt that some of the things that he said was real. I admired the fact that he spoke such realness with seemingly little attachment. I aspired to be that way, especially being in the position I was in, where the people aren't attached to the very peoples' vote they are trying to get. I went into to the office the next day for the meeting, as I would any day, and was greeted with the same smug that I'd be greeted with everyday. Daily, my distaste was progressing, with the zenith occurring on this day. Ryan asked me if we could set up a rally at the community center, which I thought was a wonderful idea. However, when Ryan secretly mentioned that he may want to tear the facility down to replace it with his new office, as mayor, I was stunted. Again, I felt used. I felt as if my ideas were being used against the community that belonged to in order to ultimately foil them. Still in silence, I walked away and asked the Cleavers if we could use it, and then went on to explain Ryan's plan. I told them, not to worry, though, I had a plan.

The day of the rally came, and I noticed Ryan looking at the community center like a lion looks at its prey just before they eat it. Calm, cool and collected, I made sure that things ran smoothly, because it was about to get rough. Ryan looked at me with a face of approval before he stepped to the podium to talk about how I felt. When he spoke, the people reacted with as warm a response as they would have to their own, probably because it was the thoughts of their own. It felt like butterflies were mating in my stomach as Ryan wrapped up and I stepped forward. I thought about the dude I saw on pro wrestling the night before when I grabbed the microphone. "Elvis Pressley, the 'King of Rock –n – Roll'. Christopher Columbus, the man who 'discovered' this great nation." These men have a couple of things in common. The first is that they are revered in American history, the second is that they are well known for something they really didn't do, just like the man sitting to my left." I could see select members of the audience's eyes get big in shock, but I had already let this pipe bomb go, so I figured I continue. "Columbus, the grand father of this country, was known as the man who discovered it. But allow me to propose this question: how ca you discover something if someone has already been there? I mean there were Native Americans here that he and his pilgrims drove out after they welcomed them in." Ryan's head dropped in disbelief as I continued. "That's an injustice. Elvis Pressley, the hip swinging sex symbol known as the King of Rock – n – Roll, carried an act that really wasn't his. In fact his songs were written and performed by African Americans, you know, the one's who were only good for shinning his shoes. And now, to this man to my left, who had a taste of the inner –city in working at a school, but quite frankly chose not to hang. He admitted to me that he doesn't relate, which is not an issue, however, his actions as of late have showed me that he doesn't want to. This man just wants to sit on his high horse, with his black girlfriend to say to the people 'Hey, I'm hip with you', just so that he can get your vote. Let me ask you, how many of you enjoyed the things that he told you here today? How many of you felt that he totally hit the nail right on the head with his comments? How many of you felt that those plans couldn't have been written better by one of your own? Well, that's because they were written by one of your own. I wrote those comments and I am sorry that I allowed Elvis Pressley to convey them before he could get the chance to Christopher Columbus us. The truth is, we need a mayor that understands the people, and doesn't have to relate to each one of the them. We need a person who actually cares enough to tell us the truth. We need a mayor who fights for this city, and does things that will reach everyone." The crowd roared as I walked off stage and eventually away from the rally. Ryan stormed away from the stage with his administration in shear frustration. I walked away with half of the crowd following me to shake my hand and encourage me. I felt a huge burden lifted off of my shoulders, like an emotional sigh of relief. I walked all the way home, opened the door and plopped on the couch, with somewhat of a surreal sense for what had just taken place.

PART 2

▼

Chapter 1

"Black President"

• • • • • • •

Days had gone by since the rally, but it seemed as though the events had still been fresh in people's minds. I had become a local celebrity, somewhat of a hero in my community. People would constantly stop me to shake my hand or just to talk to me, like they would the President. I wasn't used to this type of attention from people outside of my family, so this was definitely a new and relatively uncomfortable feeling. I mean, there's just something about going to the supermarket and not being able to buy a jug of milk without people asking you questions, that just kind of seemed off to me. It wasn't that bad though, I guess. Anyways, and on a brighter note, the results came back recently and my exposure of Ryan made the difference because he was not elected mayor. I felt a sense of accomplishment. The people were incredibly appreciative, and they constantly let me know of it. They would always tell me, "Brother, you really shed some light", or "we need your ideas in the office." I had gotten such a good rapport with the people that apparently the newly elected mayor asked me to speak at a luncheon that he was hosting. I thought long and hard about it, and eventually agreed. The Cleavers felt it would be a great chance for me get my ideas out on a larger level. They continued to remind me to "stay true to what you believe."

A few days prior to the luncheon, I got a call directly from the mayor. I found that to be odd given that we hadn't ever had a conversation, nor had we ever even met. (When I received the invitation, it came from his secretary) "Hey there, friend", the mayor stated with a degree of excitement. Feeling a little uneasy about his personal approach and given I didn't really know him well, I replied, "Hi". He then proceeded to tell me about how much he appreciated my ideas, and couldn't wait for me to speak at the luncheon, but I sensed something different. I said nothing though, just answered many of his questions with "thanks sir", and "yes". Once the conversation ended, I felt a little uneasy on the inside, I felt like that phone call was not necessarily to tell me how much he'd appreciated my thoughts. However, I brushed it off and forged ahead.

Once the day had arrived, I made certain to show up to the City Hall early, however, he wasn't there. I thought it was a bit unprofessional that the host wasn't even there early, and eventually on time, but again, I brushed it off. Once the mayor arrived he pulled me into his office for what I believed to be a pep talk. "You know, I am truly grateful for you" he said staring out of his window onto a rainy city. Curious about his gratitude, I asked why. "Son, you single handedly destroyed that Ryan kid's campaign. I mean you destroyed him. You don't even carry a political title, and you annihilated a mayoral candidate. That's impressive. I won't lie to you, I tried to get by using my natural charisma, because it seems like in politics, they look for a certain type of person. Shoot, and all the attention you get, is just awesome. Man, there are women that know that I'm married, but they still want to be with the ol' mayor. And, lets just say I don't like to let the people down. I mean, I try to make all of the right/moral decisions, but hey, I like to live a little too. I enjoy a little bit of the gonja, if you know what I mean. But anyways, it's people like us; people like you who deserve to sit in seats like this. It's people like you who deserve to be treated like royalty. It's people like you who deserve...the women. So, at this luncheon, I know you'll knock em dead, but as you look out and see all of the people, the cameras, the women, I want you to think about potentially joining the team."

After the mayor's ludicrous spew, he escorted me out to a barrage of cameras and people with suits on. I won't lie, I was impressed and for the first time in my life, I felt like I mattered. I walked through the hall with a degree of fanfare, as if these higher ups knew who I was. It was cool being seated at the head table, being waited on, as opposed to waiting on people. A sense of entitlement came over me, I mean after all, I worked hard. When the time came I delivered, if I may say so myself, and the people hung on every single word. I stepped off stage to a standing ovation, and much adoration by the people. After the luncheon ended, I was greeted by a very beautiful woman, who said that she'd enjoyed my speech and was interested in potentially "getting to know me a little better." I saw the mayor in my far sight nodding in approval. "Before you 'get to know me', do you have a boyfriend", I said jokingly, but with serious intent. (I didn't want to get burned twice) Laughing, she said, "no I don't." Feeling that I dodged a bullet I continued to talk to her, not really paying much attention to the fact that she was white. She said, "You know, you're a really compelling speaker, and I feel as if you could one day be president of the country. Imagine that. You, the leader, the man of this country."

▼

Chapter 2

"She"

· · · · · · ·

She was pretty cool, Daria was her name. She was unlike any other woman I'd ever met, she was very encouraging and genuinely interested, or so it seemed. I mean, she was always telling me how she thought I should've been this or should've been that, and I'd never had attention like that before. I relished in it too; it was nice to find someone who believes in you and your potential to be great. Anyways, she and I hung out together almost everyday, and on the days we weren't around each other, we were talking or texting. Now, you'd think that because I was so consumed with this woman that I'd be off focus, but she actually kept me focused. She actually got me a job working for the mayor, you guessed it, helping him write his speeches.

The mayor was a very interesting person, I mean, he really did seemed like he cared. I watched how he'd greet people, give young teenagers his number to call him for counseling, etc. I respected that, really, I did. I felt like "finally, we've got a mayor, a leader who actually cares about the people." I eventually forgot about that conversation that we had back at the banquet, and counted him an honorable man.

Anyways, Daria always made sure that I was meeting the deadlines, on time to all of the rallies, and visible when we were hanging out with the mayor. She was so ambitious and I thought it was pretty sexy. I mean, I'm not too in love with the looks of things, but she and I were quite the couple. Ebony and ivory, so to speak. I really felt like she added an extra dimension to me, as if she made me a better man or something. I don't know, all I do know is that we very heavy into one another. She never really bothered to ask me about my upbringings, my parents, siblings, etc, she was into who I was at that time, which made me bother weary of her, and comfortable at the same time.

One night, Daria and I went out for a night on the town. I remember that as we walked through the park swarms of people came to talk to us, well me. They asked me all types of questions, asking for autographs photos, the whole nine yards. As people walked up, I looked at Daria who was staring back with a look of satisfaction. I was confused, usually people on a date would deny the attention, but she seemed as if she embrace it. Looking at her face, I kind of perked up. I had to embrace the status, and the attention of what I had accomplished and who I was. After the fanfare subsided, Daria and I sat in the car. She said, "You are a winner. You are that talented tenth. You are somebody. You are a winner. You've made it. Enjoy who you've become. Loosen up a bit. Have some fun. Embrace it!" I took in every word she said that night, and I decided that I' whole heatedly embrace who I had become.

▼

Chapter 3

"Fitting In"

• • • • • • •

With Daria by my side, and a new found understanding for where I'd been in life, I walked and talked with a different swagger. When with the mayor I pretended I was the mayor, after all I did write many of his speeches. I walked hard; instead of trying to fit in, I simply forced my way in with the people in high places. The mayor and I had grown pretty close, and I could see that he really trusted me. So much so, that he was really himself around me.

During the summer, he invited me to this exclusive party that some of the officials hadn't even been invited to. He threw this lavish party once a year in the middle of the summer. I picked up Daria, who was dressed looking very good by the way, and she simply said, "are you ready?" A strange feeling arose in me at that point; I became nervous. When we got there, everything seemed pretty classy; there was valet parking, they was serving fruit, etc. I relaxed little as time progressed thinking, "maybe Daria was just tripping." I finally met up with the mayor, who seemed like an altogether different person. I mean, aside from the fact that he was noticeably intoxicated, he just seemed like his morals had diminished. He invited myself and Daria upstairs, where I saw some of the most disturbing images I'd ever seen. Upstairs, was where the real party was going down. I saw women sprawled all over the place; promiscuous sex and drug use seemed to be the theme of the night. To my far right I saw the mayor, entrenched in women, with his wife leading the charge. Daria looked at me with a look that crossed between satisfaction, "Have some fun. You've earned it." I had never done any type of drugs, and I didn't even like taking pills for headaches. I was shocked that the girl that I was dating actually encouraged me to have sex with another woman, right in front of her. I looked back at her with a face of confusion and curiosity, "Wha......". But before I could finish, she said, "Sweetheart, enjoy it. You've earned it. Live a little. You work so hard, and besides I like to spice things up a bit." Half curious and half reluctant, I began to indulge.

Abiding in skepticism, I took some Molly and dove in. The atmosphere had become dreary, dark and uncertain, yet lustful, spontaneous, and almost mastochistic. I felt a sense of dominance as I surfed the atmosphere. I stepped aside, let loose and allowed the drugs that had been in system to dictate where or with whom I'd end up. A part of me felt that this was wrong, but those feelings slowly weaved away as Molly slipped through my bloodstream. I had slipped into a parallel universe; one of discomfort and promiscuity, pleasure and hypocrasy. It was weird, but this was where everyone was, all of the important people at least. I had felt like a college student subjecting myself to peer pressure just to fit into the crowd. As I further engaged, I looked at Daria, and she looked back at me with a face of approval. She then knelt down and kissed me passionately. "You're one of us now," she said. The night passed me by; I was too confused to try to figure it out, but it was tantalizing to my flesh.

▼

Chapter 4

"Decisions, Decisions"

• • • • • • •

Continued to kick it with the mayor, after all he was giving political exposure. I was afraid to bring up the party to him, but after a while, I just couldn't hold it in any longer. We were hanging at his house when I finally addressed him. "Sir, what's the deal with that party?" I asked inquizatively. "Ahhh, did you enjoy?" he asked wearing a face of satisfaction. "Yeah, it was okay," I said almost reluctantly. Sensing my discomfort, the mayor said, "Son, this is politics. This is what you sign up for, when you look to get into politics. I mean, you have to politic your way into politics. It's about rubbing elbows. People in high places aren't always there because they've worked hard. They in fact have gotten there because they worked smart. By smart, I mean they were smart enough to work those folks who could do something for them." The Mayor laughed. I sported a confused look, as he continued, "Stuff like that, that's just what we do. The women, they do it to be with the guys who do it to be where we are. You've got that "it" factor. So, just consider that your initiation."

I had made it. I had somewhat reached the place that I had been longing to reach since I left college. Sure, O had done some crazy things to get there, but I was there and that was what was most important. I had represented a small percentage of people who had come from where I came from and hit it big. It was more than just making it out, it was about being somewhere and most importantly, being somebody. However, while in this state, I pondered whether this was all a mistake.

I mean, yeah, I had kind of made it to where I eventually wanted to be, but at what price? I mean, growing up the way I did, the Man was this overwhelming force that you seemingly couldn't escape. They controlled everything like taxes, your home, education, etc. And here I was, politicking with them, sitting at their tables, laughing at their whack jokes. And, craziest of all, I was deeply involved with a white woman.

A strong part of me felt as though I was selling out, like I was a turncoat of sorts. Was I supposed to be the voice for the voiceless? The mouth piece of the ghetto? The man who fought for the good of the people who I grew up in my neighborhood? On the other hand, I liked the suits, the banquets, dining with what I perceived to be kings, and all of that other stuff. I was torn between these two paths. A kid like me never grew up having the money I did, seeing the things that I've seen and being in the places that I've been since joining the mayor. The more looked at my bank account, my closet and Daria, the easier my choice became.

▼

Chapter 5

"Voicebox"

• • • • • • •

The Mayor and I had really become really tight. In a weird way, I kind of looked up to him; I saw him as a superior in a sense. The mayor had developed so much trust in me that he asked me to take his place at one of his international banquets. The Mayor had done some networking and ended up being chosen to speak at a banquet in London. He wanted to go on vacation, but he also wanted to keep the connection and positive reputation. I didn't want to go, I mean London, really? I hadn't really thought of anything outside of where we were. Sensing this, the Mayor got to me immediately. "You know, this is a really important thing for us. We could be big!" he said with excitement. Sensing that I hadn't been convinced, he continued, this time descending his tone. "One day, after a long hunting trip an old man was walking down the road came across a damaged snake. The old man, having mercy on that snake, took him in and nursed the snake to a full recovery. You know what that snake did? That snake bite the old man! In response, the old man grabbed the snake by the snack and snapped it." I sat in cold fear as he looked at me tersely. "You don't want to be that snake, do you?" he asked rhetorically. I instantly changed my mind.

As the day neared, I grew in anxiety. I had this crazy blend of optimism and pessimism, joy and sadness, courage and fear. I had spoken to Daria and she told me that she couldn't accompany me. See, she herself had some projects brewing and I always like to let my lady do her thing.

Seeing Things In Black and White

I was going in alone. It was me, a podium and the English. I sat on the plane and attempted to relax a bit, while my mind raced. There was this weird feeling that was dominant in my heart; a feeling that I had belonged. I felt like it was destiny for me to be giving this speech; these were my words and ideas after all. I was seated next to these two white women who had been looking at me flirtatiously. With Daria in my mind, I didn't plan on entertaining these women, but they were persistent. "Hi, can I help you?" I said with a mixture of sarcasm and light humor. "You could, actually..." they said snickering. I awkwardly laughed along, but was totally confused as what was actually happening. "What do you do?" they asked with a keen interest. "Well, I guess you could say that I'm in politics" I replied with a sureness. "Interesting...well! I've never really been with a black man, and you seem to be a really focused one." We're staying in our parents time share in Blackpool, perhaps you wouldn't mind spending time with us?" "Nah, but thanks for the invite." I quickly replied with a smirk. "Your loss" the second woman replied. "But you are really cute though. You know, I've never really been with a black man, and I honest have never had much interaction with blacks as a whole. I'm from a place where you'd probably think that segregation still existed. I mean, they all lived in the inner city, while we occupied the outskirts, or the suburbs if you will. We didn't necessarily go into those areas because....well, we just didn't. I don't know what it was, it's not like we didn't like each other, but it did feel like there was an underlying tension there, to be honest. I always wondered what that world was like, and if they wondered the same about us. I use to watch television and wondered if everything really was how they said it was in the ghettos. That always kid of fascinated me, and honestly, I wanted to experience it. But, I didn't think I'd be too accepted and I honestly didn't want to look like I was trying to fit in."

Something inside made me feel bad after hearing that. We talked a bit more as we flew into the night; I found the girls' to be rather interesting. We touched down in London in the wee hours in the morning. Once I got off the plane and through customs, something became immediately evident. Unlike the states, I, a black man, didn't feel ostracized. I ran into a guy wearing a black suit holding a sign that read "GOOD WILL AMBASSADOR." He glanced at me, and said,

"Are you the representa...." "Yes", I said cutting him off. "Well we are here to take to the hotel, which you'll be staying. Just follow me." I followed him outside, where there was a car waiting for me. In the car, which he drove, he asked a myriad of questions. "Do you like what you do mate?" Laughing at his accent, I answered, "Yeah." I was curious as to why he asked this question, so I asked the same question to him "Do you like what you do?" "Oh yes! I love being a chauffeur and an escort." I love doing for those who are new to my country also. I just feel as if it gives me an opportunity to serve. It's like I put the country on my back when I do so because, when guests come in, I'm the first person they come into contact with. I'm many peoples first impression of London, England. In that way, I get to serve my country. To me, that's more than fighting in the army. That's real service.

That evening, I locked myself in the room and practiced. I worked particularly on my diction; after all I needed to ensure that I was representing the Mayor the right way. I took a quick break and sat out on the balcony of my suite, which overlooked North London. I gazed out into the night, the lights, the towers, the architecture, etc. i really thought back to what the chauffeur said to mw in the car. I thought, "He's satisfied", he's happy with who is he is and what he does. He's takes driving people around seriously! He undertakes the burden of being a a representative of his country, though his seemingly minute job." For some odd reason, that really stood out to me. Taking a seat at the table, I plopped down, seemingly sinking into the chair. I was overseas, alone, representing my country in a position that I felt I was born to be in. I reflected on all of the speeches I had written for both Ryan and the Mayor. I recalled every idea I had shared, every emotion that I had put on paper for someone else to emotionlessly convey and profit from. this was my time. my chance to stand before some important people, and tell the, what was up. Then again, why does all they think even matter. What does all of this accomplish? The more politics, the better relationship, the better relationship, the more butt kissing, the more butt kissing, the more... money.

It also hit me that I had a voice, but my voice was spilling through the mouths of others. Why did I need to be writing speeches for someone else, when could've been doing it for myself? Why couldn't I be accepted for my ideas? Like Ryan, the Mayor only wanted me for what I could do for him, and thought he could just stuff money in my mouth to satisfy me... and it worked.

The good book tells us that the love of money is the root of all evil, a root that has produced a tough trunk and some firm branches. That was only half the story though; for some odd reason, a man always feels that he needs to make sure that he shows the world how big his ego is. This is a man's downfall, well, that and female persuasion. Its surprising to me how man is often easily persuaded by woman. Ever since the beginning, with Adam and Eve, a man's soft spot can usually be tied to a woman. I watched my life take the turn it did, through all of these key factors. As I continued to consider these things, a tear formed in the corners of my eyes. I had broken. I finally become honest with myself realizing that I was living a lie. I was on a power trip, and I really had no power. I was puppet, but unlike Pinnochio, I was in fact fed lies and somehow tried to breed truth. However, despite all of the wrong that had taken place, I had still operated in some form of right; I was a voice.

▼

Chapter 6

Footprints

· · · · · · ·

I had a great week with the fine folks across the pond; the hospitality was impeccable. Oh, and the speech was a home run too. many people were shaking my hand and telling me things like, "One day, you'll be a great leader," and "you're truly a great representation of your countrymen." "One gentleman came over to me and even said, "When I come to the US, I am visiting your city first." Apparently, the Mayor, had given our city a great name, and himself for that matter. The food was cool too; first time eating fish and chips unusual, but a great cultural experience nonetheless.

I was escorted back to the airport with the same gentleman who had escorted me to the hotel. He gave me a handshake and slapped in my hand a keepsake. It was a small rock. I was flustered as to why he handed this to me, and so I asked, "What's this and why are you giving it to me?" He smirked and replied, "Remember, a building is nothing more than a ton of rocks." Instead of analyzing this, which really made no sense to me, I just took the rock and shook his hand.

As my plane took off, I bid farewell to the UK, a great place indeed; a place of revelation, and resolution for me. All I could think about was the night prior to the banquet. The night I sat atop North London in the coolest suite in town. The night I gazed over bright lights, of a big city. The night I reflected, the night saw the world I lived in for what it was.

They say that the ride back always seems shorter than the ride going, and that was certainly the case here. We pulled into the airport and to my surprise, the Mayor was standing there...with Daria? I was too tired and already suffering from jet lag, so I really didn't want to hear what the boss had to say. I strolled hastily through the airport hoping to find the the train before the Mayor and Daria found me. I felt a soft hand caress my lower back accompanied by "Hey there...I missed you." Throwing her arms around my neck and jumping into my arms, was Daria. "Hey, how are you," I replied trying to mask my disinterest. "We've been waiting for you...well, more importantly, I have been waiting for you," she added seductively. "Good sir!" The Mayor interjected from seemingly out of nowhere. "I heard you really knocked it out of the park over there." He added. "Yeah, I guess", I added nonchalantly. "Well, let's head back to my office, I want to hear more about this excursion."

We headed back to the Mayor's office, and as tired as I was, I just couldn't sleep, knowing that I was working for a politician. A real politician. A person who is not only political by occupation, but political by nature. This was my dream and it turned out to be a nightmare. My perception of a politician was one who was the voice OF the people, but I had been saddened to realized that they were more of a voice TO the people. Politicians don't care about the common man, they care about the man that can do something for them. They don't care about the single mothers, they care about the trophy wives and the potentials. All that I had done for people like Ryan, who I handed the ideas of the people to, and without caring, he spit out my words verbatim, giving false hope to a people who really need it. He had no plans on doing any of it, he used me to inform him of what they wanted to hear, and even had me write it out, so that in return, he could get their vote. And now, I find myself in the same situation, a speech writer, a think tank for someone who really didn't care about people, or at least people who could not directly do anything for him. my whole London excursion was all about how an international influence could help my boss achieve his sick, tainted goals.

We pulled up in front of the City Hall and I was feeling incredibly uncomfortable. I eased my way in, contemplating whether or not I should quit, or hang in until things change. "I can't do this anymore" I said as soon as we sat down. "Son, come on, be serious," The Mayor replied downplaying my statement. "I found it interesting that instead of asking where this all came from, he just went ahead and tried to downplay my thought. "I really can't do this, sir" I added adamantly." Sensing my seriousness, the mayor responded, "Why?" "I'm burnt out, sir, and I don't think that I want to remain in this profession anymore." I said with genuine sadness.

The Mayor just looked at me, as if he could see what was inside of my head or something. "So, what are you going to do? And before you answer, consider all of the luxuries I've exposed you to. All of the suits I placed on your back, all of the vacation time I'm responsible for. Remember the fame that I brought to you. Remember the fact that the "big people" know your name because of me." In genuine disgust, I got up looked at the Mayor and said, "I'm out."

He looked like I had betrayed him. He looked like a Mortal Kombat character just after Shang Tsung takes their soul from them. Realizing that I was serious, he turned and faced the window. I walked out of the room and breathed a sign of relief. Then, out of nowhere, I heard the chime of broken glass on a desk. I turned back in, and found the mayor of the floor with broken glass in his hand and a cut across his shirt. "Mr. Mayor are you okay? What just happened?" I asked frantically. "Oh, I'm fine, just a little accident, that's all. Can you do me a favor, can you call my security guards?" He responded in anguish. "Searching for the phone, I replied, "Sure". He urged me that all was well, but didn't want me to wrap him, and I was a bit confused about that considering the huge gashes he has on his hand and across his chest. The guards came about five minutes later and in a stroke of both genius and fraudulence, he shouted to his guards, "This man has assaulted me and I'm bleeding." I had been betrayed.

The guards wrestled me to the ground, restraining me and then kicking me with great force. These guys were all well over six feet, and well over about 270 pounds, give or take. It was like being jumped by five offensive lineman and they had the nerve to be wearing boots. Once they had literally gotten their kicks out, they picked my battered, beaten and borderline bloodied body up and took me outside, where, from what I remember, we took a ride to the jailhouse.

I had been betrayed on cue, it seemed, and I was facing a major penalty for not complying with the mayor's wickedness. A man I had once looked up to, had revealed himself as simply that, a man, but moreso, a politician. It seemed that I had gotten what it was I asked for, the opportunity to be in politics, but politics had somehow gotten in the way. It makes sense to me now as to how people can enter into a position where they are responsible for making decisions for other people, and ultimately end up becoming, dare I say it, politicians. I'm sure that at one point the mayor had good intentions, but money, attention, and power probably crept in and he became a politician. I wish I could end this story at that point, but the story continued....

▼

Chapter 7

"Black-Male"

• • • • • • •

I sat in the jail cell completely depleted of all emotion, when the mayor showed up. He entered into the cell with somewhat of an insolent look on his face, and closed the door behind him, never taking his eyes off of me. He stared at me, as if I had wronged him, as if he was awaiting some sort of apology. I just stared back, emotionlessly, waiting for him to speak. "You know son, you really screwed yourself here. You're are the reason why you're sitting here with bruises on your face, and bloodstains on your shirt. Not me, I did nothing to you." He paused and stared at me. "As a matter of fact, I did do something for you. I gave you an opportunity. I took you under my wing, and gave you an opportunity to be great. And what did you do? you stabbed in the back." I sat flustered and confused as he continued. "Your job was to be the right hand man, of THE MAN. I run this town...I'm the Mayor. All you had to do was handle my business. But no, you have to do you own thing, you have to develop a little ego. Well allow me to let you in on a little secret... there's only room for one ego in this town and that ego is mine", he reminded me. He began a slow saunter around the room, "This city, is my universe. Mine. I own it. Before me, this city was a step above a wasteland, but since my ascension, this city has experienced one of the greatest turnarounds in history. So, these people, YOU, all of you owe me." As he continued to aggrandize himself, I listened. I started at the bottom of the barrel, just like you did. I began as somebody's intern, and I was generally happy to be somewhere. But I wanted more, I wanted to ascend all the way to the top of the food chain. And I've done that. I've made my way to the top, and I refused to go back. I won't allow people like you to taint my image, to destroy the positive perceptions that I've created. I've single handedly put this place on the map. I did before I became the Mayor, and when I got into office, I finished a great work."

I listened in complete disgust before I eventually tuned him out completely. I checked back in however, once he said to me, "Remember the story of that snake? Huh? Remember that snake who was taken in by the old fella on the side of the road? Well, I'm willing to keep you on board, but you have some proving, and some making up to do." I thought back to that snake story, and how it related to me. I wasn't picked up on the side of the road, I wasn't just tossed off to the side, I wasn't a wounded animal when I met the mayor. Finally breaking my silence, I said, "Yeah, I remember that story, and the truth is, you're that snake. It was in fact me that picked you up off the side of the road," I said with a certain disregard in my voice. "Have it your way, son. But, your way, will cost you," He concluded. He left the jail cell signaling to the guards, another beating was about to commence. After being beat up for most of the night, I was released, well, more so thrown to the grounds outside of the door the following morning. I went by the train station, and eventually spotted a copy of the Daily News, which had a photo of me being taken away from City Hall. When you're the Mayor of this city, you control the city, and the way people see the city. The propaganda you project, is what people will receive about you and your city, it becomes their impression, their perception. It must be great to have that type of power, to basically tell the world what's best for them, and what they should think. What is sad about this is that he really does have the pull that he says he does. The headline of the article read, "TURNCOAT TAKEDOWN" with the subhead reading, "Mayor Withstands Beating."

"Great", I thought. The mayor had successfully painted the portrait of a criminal, a monster, and a snake in the grass. I walked with my head down because I had seen my dream of being successful, working in politics become the biggest disappointment of my life. It was all I lie; it was politics, essentially. I couldn't believe that all that I had worked for wasn't what I'd envisioned it to be. I felt like a kid on Christmas who didn't get what he'd been asking for all year long.

PART 3

▼

Chapter 1

"The Inside Out"

• • • • • • •

I didn't feel the need to take a train, bus or cab, so I decided I'd walk home. As I took the walk home, I had reflected on the events that had taken place; Daria, those English girls on the plane, the plateau that I had reached in local politics, and the Mayor of course. As I walked home, despite feeling my lowest, I couldn't help but feel optimistic, in spite of the pessimistic circumstances I was surrounded by. The time seemed to fly as before I knew it, I had approached my apartment building, in which there seemed to be much commotion. I saw things being moved in and out of the building, and as I approached the door, which had been propped open by the movers, I was met by a familiar face who appeared to remember me. She was a petit white woman wearing what looked to be an expensive, wool trench coat. The sound of her heels clicking against the cement pavement became more and more audible as I had gotten closer to her. "Uuhhh.... hey!" She said somewhat excitedly. "Hey..." I replied half puzzled and half caring. "You don't remember me, do you?" She said somewhat disappointed. I shook my head in shame, assisted by a smirk plastered across my face, "Nah, but your face looks very familiar." "Remember me from the interview? At the university a few years ago?" She replied. I instantly went back to the babbling, teenager like, young lady, whose story flat out annoyed me that day, "Oh, yes, I do remember you! What are you doing here?" "Well, I'm moving in. It seemed like a very cool area, and I was curious Remember that job that we both went for? Well, I've been there since and within months I was moved up. They said that my face was doing wonders for the school, and that practically every family that I sold to, ended up committing their children to the school. It was easy work for me. I ended up working my way up to a managerial role and eventually became a supervisor. When I saw what I was making, I was like, well, I don't have to live with mom and dad anymore in the burbs, so I thought I'd move down here, to be a little closer to the action, and well...civilization." She said with a chuckle. "So, what are you doing here?" I paused and looked at her with a raised eyebrow wondering if actually wanted to tell her that I lived there, with fears that she'd possibly bug me or ask a ton of questions about the area. However, I did want her to know that I was doing well, so I replied, "I actually live here. I work in politics too, I'm... well, was close to the Mayor of city, and so I realized I needed to get out... you know, move to a better part of town, something closer to City Hall." I wore a false pride as I said that, because uncertainty had been plaguing my existence at this point. I bid farewell as I went into the hectic lobby, which was swamped with bags, furniture and people moving in what seemed to be clusters. I managed to get through the mess of movers and hit the elevator, as the only thing on my mind at this point, is getting into my bed and sleeping this nightmare away. I begin taking my keys out of my pocket as I approach my door... which had a Sheriff's notice on it. That ounce of optimism I felt, quickly turned into rage as I immediately picked upon the phone to call management. In short, they didn't disclose why I was being evicted, they just urged me to remove my things and evacuate the premises by the end of the day.

I thought that being beat up by the cops, and humiliated in the newspaper was bad, but this was another level.

I couldn't sit down and think because I didn't have time to, I needed to find somewhere to stay first. I had been living on the good side of time for quite some time and had gotten use to being here. I didn't know anyone who lived in the area, so I was pretty much going to have to move somewhere else. After sifting through the dozens of people that I had known, some of which were no where to be found, I had one option... I had to call my brother. He stayed in the house we grew up in, and was holding down a job to keep the lights on. I called him, and left a message on his voicemail:

"Little brother, listen I'm going to need to move back into the house. Some crazy stuff went down, and I'm out of this apartment. Anyways, I need you to call me ASAP because I have to leave now."

Minutes turned into hours as I sat and waited for my brother to call me back. It was just after noon, and I needed to make a move. I sat on my sofa and surveyed the room for a final time, knowing that I'm probably going to have to give up a life that I wanted for so long. I thought, "How could I possibly go back home? This was the life I dreamed of and now, it's all over. My job is done with the Mayor, I don't have much saved because I lived fast... basically, I have nothing to show for all that I left home for. I left as what I perceived as a hero, and now I'm back to square one." I called my brother three to four more times as the day progressed. Its early evening, and I let time slip away as I dwelled pensively in the battleground of my mind. Frustrated, I texted him in all caps, "CALL ME NOW!!!"

Immediately I received a text back:
"Hey big bro. Ain't heard from you in a minute. What's the move?"

Pissed isn't even a good enough adjective to describe my feelings. I texted him, telling him to call me and when he did, the first thing I wanted to know was why he didn't text me back. "Big bro, don't nobody do them calls no more. You gotta text people now in days. They see that immediately and can screen whether it's really important or not." I didn't get it, but I didn't have time to analyze it, it was early evening and I needed to go. I explained my plight, and my need to get out at that moment, and thankfully, he had a friend who owned a truck. We quickly ended the conversation and he was on his way. I knew I needed to start moving things, but was a bit embarrassed that I had to move out. I sort of didn't want my neighbors to see me leaving, fearing that they'd think I couldn't pay my rent or something, or that I was just another black statistic.

But I had to go though...

When my brother arrived at the building, he parked right in front so we could swiftly move my things out. We stuffed everything both on the lift and in the back of the truck. In short, we were able to get everything out in under an hour, (Hey, it was a bachelor pad) and I chose not to look back at what I was leaving. It wasn't just a nice building, on a nice side of town, it represented my dream, and a lifestyle I wanted to create for myself. My brother looked around in sheer amazement, "wow... you really messed up bro. This place is dope." I grabbed him by the arm, as his statements reinforced what I had already felt, and shoved him out of the door. We walked out of the building and he continued, "This neighborhood is dope too. You know, I never thought you would live in a place like this. You know we typically don't get to this side of town...." As my brother made that comment two police officers who were riding down the block, stopped directly in front of us, "You fellas lost?" "No," I responded, "we are just going to our truck to leave." He looked at us, then looked over at our truck and with a smile replied, "Good." They drove off and we were honestly, just grateful to make it out alive, let alone not in the back of their car.

The car ride home was a quiet one, especially considering all that I had experienced in the last year. My mind was still filled with questions on how all seemed to have fallen apart for me. My train of thought derailed as halfway through the ride home, my brother finally broke the ice, "Bro, when we get home, you probably won't recognize some things. It all started right after you left... youngn's just started wildin' out. People were seemingly getting shot like every weekend man. It wasn't safe. It got so bad, that Mr. Cleaver told me that he was considering sliding. Parents started coming to the schools instead of having the kids walk home... man it was just different. Then, I remember one weekend, we started seeing cop cars on the corner of our block. Then, it wasn't just our block, it was the next block, then the next, and so on. Cops was out here asking questions, circling the Chinese store, all types of stuff. But you know what's crazy, all that shooting, fell off. It started to become a little bit safer. Kids started walking to school again, the vibe felt a little more chill. Now, across town, that was another story. But one of my boys told me that the same thing started happening over there. It's like the cops are focusing on our neighborhood or something. Either way though, it's gonna feel a lot safer once we get there, watch.

The only thing that made me smile on this long day was seeing the house that I grew up in. It wasn't the luxury apartment near City Hall with amenities, but it was home. I stepped out of the truck with a smile as we immediately started unpacking. I kind of couldn't wait until the next day, when everyone was out, so that I could catch up with many of the folks that I'd grown up with and those that had seen me grow up. Though I was embarrassed that I felt that I had essentially failed, at least I was back home. As I stepped back outside to grab the last bag of clothes, the feeling of joy quickly transformed into one of uneasiness as I looked across the street and noticed a few things: a new family in a new house that looked as if it was built totally different than the others on the block, in a place where an old friend of mine used to live. I knew this was a new family because I was able to see the inside of their home as there were no curtains or blinds up. It was unusual to see a white family in our neighborhood. I didn't let my eyes move while I called my brother to the door. "Hey, what happened to the Little's?" He responded seemingly without hesitation, "Oh, they said somebody bought they crib, they handed them and check and they dipped."

▼

Chapter 2

"The Outside In"

· · · · · · ·

I woke up the next morning feeling great to have been home, but still a bit uneasy about what I was told by my brother regarding our old friends. I mean, I had no issue that there was a new family, let alone a white family, but how it went down was a bit of an issue to me. I got out of the house early to see what the neighborhood felt like during the morning rush. It was different, but something about it felt familiar. I walked by the elementary school, greeted by the chaotic sounds of screaming children, and scrambling parents. The impatient beeping of horns from the parking lot reminded me of my childhood, and growing attending this very school. I stopped and stared at the madness for a bit, as it struck up something inside of me. The same feeling I received while working with Ryan and even the Mayor, were drawn up again. I looked at many of those kids, in their innocence, and saw myself; someone that didn't know that he didn't know. I remembered how I saw so few faces that looked like me, which inadvertently had an impact on me. Some years back, I did try to fight to make education a thing again in our neighborhood, but I liked the allure of politics, but maybe I was on to something in the beginning. At that moment, I heard a familiar voice say, "Hey stranger!" I turned around, and to my surprise, I was the Mr. Cleaver. "What's up there greatness!" He replied, as I turned and reach for a handshake. "Hey, I'm just trying to follow in your footsteps OG!" I answered shaking his hand firmly. "What are you doing here?" I added. "Welp, you know my grandson goes here. He's in the 3rd. He seems to like the school, but lately he's been coming home with some questions. Said that this year he'd been seeing more and more white kids, which was different than what he was used to." He leaned against the fence with his eyes gazing across the school yard, adding, "You know the old neighborhood, we used to black folk and out Latino cousins. For a kid who saw that most of his young life, to now be seeing whites, it is a bit of a culture shock for him...but hey, he likes it, and I think it's alright too." We both were quiet as the children went inside for school, when he turned to me and asked, "So, what's all that jive with the Mayor. I was hearing about something in the newspaper. You got caught up in some mess." I just looked at him with a blank stare, and shook my head. "Yeah, it didn't sound like you. Anyway, what you doing? Like, you got a job lined up?" I shook my head indicating "no" in shame. "I don't have anything, but I need something. I feel like the newspaper ad is going to mess my stock up in terms of trying to do something constructive to society." I said. Mr. Cleaver looked at me and said, "The school is actually hiring." I glanced quickly at him with a raised eyebrow as he continued, "Yeah, they reached out to us to have some flyers placed around the community center. The thing is, ain't nobody too interested in working in a school, and with the way the hood is changing, I don't know if that will change. Let's take a little walk."

We started walking down the block towards the community center, and many of the differences Cecil talked about, echoed in Mr. Cleaver's conversation. "Look at these houses. You got all this new construction out of nowhere. Then, next thing you know, families that done been here 30, even 40 years, are gone. When you left this place was crime ridden, but it spiked even more after you left. It was to the point, where we couldn't do nothing. The cops started actively patrolling the area, and the crime chilled out. Of course that entailed getting rid of people they though might have dealing, and targeting suspicious folks, but the crime pretty much halted. Then, these houses just popped up." He pointed at two houses across from the community center that stood out, towering over the rest like your middle and ring fingers tower over your others, colored green, which was a stark contrast to the others on the block. He added, "And after the first two, which nobody could afford to buy at first, there were a few others that started popping up. Once the first few were bought, it was a wrap. A lot of folks were either offered out, or just couldn't afford to stay. You know this area is full of renters, so the landlords were just like, 'let's move the price, because at this point we can.' The neighborhood started to improve, the whole nine. And this is why you see a more diversified elementary school, than the one you graduated from. But, as long as my grandson can live in a safer place, I'm good."

I didn't know how to feel.

On one hand, my neighborhood was safer, while on the other, families were leaving, etc. Despite that. I knew that I needed a job, and that job at the school sounded tasty. I asked Mr. Cleaver if I could use the computer while I was there to send in my application. He allowed me to, and even agreed to plug me in when he went by the school to pick up his grandson. We sat and chatted a bit more about the state of the community center, and the neighborhood in general. Around noon, I bid him farewell and walked back home. By the time I got in, my brother had stopped at home on a break from his job. "Hey big bro, did you start looking for gigs?" He asked inquisitively. "Yeah, heard out old school was hiring, so I thought I'd apply." I replied somewhat nonchalantly. "Yeah man, cause um, these bills are tripping. The rent went up, and the landlord ain't hearing no sob-story. As long as we been renting from him, now all of a sudden he's switching up. Plus, my job is pretty much dead end at this point and I've been struggling to find anything that's willing to pay me anything more than like $15 an hour. They never told me that you can't maintain on that type of wage, and still have a life. It's cramping my style bro." I listened to his soliloquy and felt a bit more uneasy about all I had been hearing. Even though I was home, I was in some bizarre world which was increasingly unwinding before me.

My brother left for work, while I sat and home and surveyed the changes.

▼

Chapter 3

"The Interview Pt. 2"

· · · · · · ·

Just after my brother left, I received a phone call from one of the school officials. I answered to a familiar sounding woman's voice on the other end asking me the soonest I could get in to for an interview. Considering that I wasn't really doing anything, I ensured her that i could come in the following day. So, just like that, within a matter of hours I had an interview set up. I sat around for a bit watching television, something I hadn't really had much time to do for some time. Lodged between a bunch of commercials advertising local lawyers on a local television station was an ad for the Mayor. To say it was a political statement, is a supreme understatement. The commercial depicted him as a family man, and as a man for the people. There shots of him sitting with his wife and children at a barbecue, as family members sat around laughing and seemingly having a great time. It made me sick. Considering I had never met his wife, and was certain he didn't have children this level of annoyance this ad inflicted on me was exceptionally high. I turned the television off as I was completely turned off by the commercial.

Sometime later, I was down the basement grabbing some cleaning products to clean my room up. I stumbled upon a can full of photos; the same can that my brother had discovered some years ago. I brought the can upstairs and dumped all of the pictures on my bed. Sifting through the pictures, many of myself as a child. As I examined each picture, I was brought back to many of the moments. I saw a child, who didn't know that he didn't know. A kid who didn't understand the conditions that he abode in. It made me smile. I grabbed a handful of pictures to dump back into the can when I noticed a small picture fall out. Surveying the picture, I saw Mr. and Mrs. Cleaver in handcuffs, pinned on the hood of a police car with a concerned look plastered across their faces. Their eyes were fixed on the ground, on which appeared to be a woman. I examined the picture for a bit, before placing it in my wallet and taking the full can back downstairs.

It's time for the interview, and I honestly didn't know how to feel. There were a million things on my mind, and it seemed like getting a job was just a matter of finding a number in the annals of my mind. I put on my best cloths, or what I had left of them, and took the walk down to the junior high school. It was a little after school had begun, so the area was desolate of humanity, aside from a small late population of students and parents. I made my way into the school, and was surprised at the changes.... or lack thereof. Essentially the school looked exactly like it did when I left, close to 2 decades ago. The walls still contained the yellowish, stained-looking brick, complete with a cream color painted overcoat. The floors were waxed, but still contained many of the cracks that my friends and I sought to avoid, as we thought they'd break our mother's backs. The front office still looked the same, as the hectic nature instantly took me back to times having to report here as a child. The sound of staples clamping the edge of paper, provided a baseline for the of voices seemingly overlapping each other as secretaries, and school officials held separate conversations. As I entered the office and sat down, I somehow heard a familiar voice over the chaos, but didn't see the face. It as coming from the principal's office, in which my interview was to be held. I looked in that direction, attempting to see I could match the face to the voice, when I noticed the door was being held slightly ajar by one of the secretaries who was speaking to the principal, while standing halfway out of the door. She then turned, and quickly scanned the office, squinting her eyes slightly as if she was looking for someone. Then she locking in on me, after which she walked over to me. She approached me, smiling, "You must be here for the interview. The Principal is waiting for you in the back." I nodded my head, and accompanied it with a smile as I headed to the back. Being led to the back by the secretary I looked around, and noticed that as I looked at every desk titled, "Assistant Principal," there was a white face attached to it. I quickly shrugged it off, and continued to the Principal's office. After walking past a sea of white faces, I entered the Principal's office as was greeting a black one. The familiar voice I heard, had a face attached to it that I recognized. It was Ryan's girlfriend, whom I met at the school district office, just before I started working with him. I was certain that I was dead. I had embarrassed her boyfriend in front of our entire community, and I'm almost certain his campaign tanked as a whole on account of me. I did what I felt was right, and I wasn't going to apologize for it, so I suppressed my fear, instead wearing a sense of bravado. Before I could open my mouth to formally greet her, she opened the conversation with,

"... I saw you the other day with Mr. Cleaver, standing at the gate and I remembered your face. See, I linked up with them shortly after we met... remember you told me you worked with them? Well, I reached out to them shortly after you started working with the Mayor and they helped me get here. They had an entire campaign out to make me Principal! The school board had no choice at that point, they had to put me in. You know, I drew a lot of inspiration from your passion for better schools in our area and when I saw you, I shot a simple text to Mr. Cleaver telling you to apply. I didn't want him to tell you that I wanted you in particular because I wasn't sure you remembered my name, and I didn't want to startle you by saying that 'The Principal of the School would like to speak to you...' as I wasn't sure of your feelings on getting back into education. We all kind of saw how things ended with you and the Mayor, and I honestly wasn't sure I'd see your face, or if you'd be up to being around in any way. But, I'm glad your here. This isn't so much an interview as it is me asking you to come aboard. I remembered your fervor, and how much you cared... and I need that here. I feel that you'd be an asset to our staff, actually, I know that you'd be an asset to my staff. I absolutely want you here. Please, come aboard."

As she spoke, I sensed a genuine urgency in her voice. This wasn't about filling a position, there something deeper at work here. "You got me." I said staring back at her. I didn't know why, I didn't understand the feeling, that weird blend of optimism and pessimism that sat at the base of my stomach like a heavy object in water. I didn't ask about salary, even though that was one of the main reasons for me being there in the first place, when she replied, "Thanks. This place will be better for you."

She then got up and began walking toward the door while quickly gesturing to me that I follow long. "Let's take a little tour around the building, I want to acquaint you with somethings." I followed closely and listened with the greatest intent as she elaborated on various aspects of the school. The first place she showed me was the office, stating, "When I came in, they were here. Honestly, I don't mind them, but it feels a little weird having a school in our context and have all these faces that don't quite look like them." I nodded awkwardly, as left the main office and headed into a hallway filled with classrooms. There were five classrooms down the main hallway, each with a different color outside of the room seemingly decorated by the students themselves. There were a group of students walking down the main stairwell moving into the "Green" classroom. The Principal stopped a few of these students and began speaking to them, "This is one of our new teachers, you'll be seeing him around soon. I wanted to show your classroom, would you mind showing us around." "No problem!" The student replied. We followed them closely into a very neat, well organized, and seemingly very cooperative classroom. Students had immediately gotten seated, and quietly began working. The noise generated from the sound of shoes squeaking across the waxed floor, transformed into pencils moving across the paper. The class was pretty diverse, there were about 28 kids in the classroom, and of that number there were about fifteen white students, nine Black students, three Puerto Rican students, and one Asian student. I thought back to what Mr. Cleaver's grandson said, and thought it was pretty cool having diversity in our area. It wasn't really something that I was used to, but I guess it was okay. I could also admit to being a bit narrow minded when it came to matters like that, as I wasn't exposed to different races until I left for school. Maybe it was nice that they were getting this social education so early. "Good morning Mrs. Kelly!" The students said as the timer went off signaling the end of the 'Warm Up' period. Mrs. Kelly was the 6th grade teacher for the "Green" Classroom. She was a short, slender, brunette with a somewhat stern disposition. I could tell by the way her classroom looked she valued order. I observed her interactions with students as she went around to check work; she was critical, a bit cold, but demanding of them. "She's demanding. I'm not the biggest fan of her attitude, but kids test well in her room." The Principal said interrupting my thinking. "She's thorough, she's incredibly detailed, and uses data to ensure that they do well. I made sure she stayed in this classroom. I think she's good for them."

We headed out of her classroom and moved down the hall a bit further, passing two other classrooms. The Principle opened the door to one of the "Red" classrooms, where we were met with a student's coat on the floor at the door. The room was a bit different, to say the least. The room wasn't quite as clean as the "Green" Classroom, and the audio in the room was a bit different as well. Whereas the "Green" Classroom was squeaky clean, quiet and well organized, the "Red" Classroom greeted us with floor marks indicative of hardcore sneaker play. The sound, in contrast to the quiet serenity of the other room, was as noisy and chaotic as the New York Stock Exchange. The teacher, Mrs. Lincoln, was a tall, thin blonde who seemed unbothered by what was taking place. She was talking at the board, but no kids were listening. As I tried watched her map out math the problems, I was distracted by two kids slap boxing in the front two seats as other kids shouted, egging them on. I was surprised, as the Principal did nothing. She sat and watched with a smirk that projected both disgust, and optimism simultaneously. We stood at the door, watching the chaos ensue when she said, "this is why I need you here." She looked sharply at me and said, "Do you notice anything different about this group?" I honestly hadn't at that point as I gazed across the room to a sea of solely black faces. "No... not really..." I said. She smirked and replied, "Good answer..."

Chapter 4

"Colors Pt. 1"

• • • • • • •

The next day I sat with the Principal to go over the curriculum. She handed me two packets; one was the state curriculum, and the other was her personally modified version. Let's take a moment to go through these two because they may seem a bit similar, but they're totally different in actuality. The state curriculum was bland, and relatively basic. It included texts that I remembered reading in high school which included the Shakespeare's, T.S. Elliot, etc. "So, what do you think about these?" She asked. "Well, honestly, I didn't really connect much with these in high school. Like, I understood that it's important to know, but I didn't actually care about any of it. It made reading tedious for me, and because of that, that's how I equated reading." I replied. "Exactly. Many of our students equate reading with boredom, because they haven't been introduced to things that peal to them. They haven't found anything that reaches into their world, so they see reading as being out of their world. We have to find a way to reach into their context... to make them care about it... which will make it easier when they encounter the Shakespeare's of the world. So that's why I propose we work with this one." She handed me the second one, which included an intro to Frederick Douglass. I was instantly intrigued. "Come on, let's take a look at it in action." She said, as she got up and led my back out through the office into the quiet hallway. "I've begun pushing this into the green classroom, and they seemed to be relatively receptive.... at least from what I've heard." she added. We walked into the classroom to the students having what appeared to be classroom debate. The room was split in half, almost opera style, as students were students seated on both sides with two podiums brought in to add to the feel. We walked into the middle of the debate as one student was making his argument:

"Our current event debate is on gentrification, which has a bad feel when say the word. It is connected to negative feelings, and people seem to have real problems with it. But, as I sat and thought about this topic, I thought we could look at it differently. I see it as improving a community. Think about it? What's really wrong with building houses on lots and over abandoned houses that nobody was using anyways. My family actually came from the suburbs to this area because it was easier for my dad to get to work. He works downtown and he found a house here in the area with new renovations and everything. It was easier, and he learned that this school was much better in test scores. It just made sense. My dad said, 'the neighborhood is getting much better, so let's move here before it gets too expensive!'"

The second student stepped up to the podium facing the first student.

"Ron is right. There is nothing wrong with improving a neighborhood. I grew up in this neighborhood, and I've been in this school since Kindergarten, I mean (sarcastically) I didn't have a choice. But I do say that this is a great thing, that the neighborhood is getting better. It's cleaner and stuff, and I even see people walking they dogs, which I never really seen before. I mean, it's just dope. Me and my friends.... oh, wait, my friends can't enjoy it like I do, because they had to move out their place. My grandma, who lived here for decades, say she can't afford the taxes or something. Next thing you know, she got to move into an apartment across town. See, the problem is not the improvement, it's the way we got to it. We got to it by getting rid of people. We got here by changing the vibe. Now, my neighborhood don't feel the same. It don't feel like home. And if you call dibs with no blinds on the windows and dog poop all over the street improvement, then I'll pass.

The first student quickly refuted,

"This is improvement. You wouldn't need improvement of something wasn't messed up in the beginning."

The second student interjected quickly...

And that's the problem. The people that think like that, always assume it's a problem."

The Principal and I both looked at each other and nodded with approval. We stayed a bit longer before heading out of the classroom and into the hallway for a debrief. As I walked out greeted by the noise projected from the classrooms next door, I got excited at the thought of having a classroom that looked, felt and functioned like that. I wanted to ask the Principal if I'd have a class like that, but it seemed she was reading my body language, because she quickly stated while looking at her clipboard, "I don't think I'll have you in a class like that." My heart sank, somewhat as she continued, "I think you'll be better suited for the orange or red group.... You can handle that, right?" "Uh... yes," I said somewhat impulsively. I really wanted what I perceived to be a well behaved group, as opposed to the madness I walked in to the previous day in the red groups room. But, as they say, beggars can't be choosers, and I needed to be working if I wanted my brother and I to stay where we were.

The next day, we went down to the red room, so I could see the group in action, as I had the weekend to plan to begin teaching on Monday morning. I thought she was taking me back to the room we had seen a few days prior, however, she kept walking, and I just sheepishly followed along. "This is your new group. 8th grade. RED. Let's go in and have them meet you." I continued to follow along, as she opened the door to a class which housed about 34, moderately toned 8th graders. When we entered, the substitute, who was seemingly hiding behind the desk, appeared elated once we walked in. He was an older guy, bald, white and spoke in a rather under confident tone. "Let's all thank Mr. Brady for subbing and taking on the mantle of being your teacher for the first Month of school." This comment was met by jeers, a "boo" and someone even laughed. "Thanks for the opportunity Principal." He stated with an elated tone. "Here's your new teacher, I'll let him introduce himself." The Principal said, placing her hands on my shoulders. Just as I went to speak, a student, "This nigga won't be here long." The class erupted into laughter, I honestly wanted to laugh as well, but I needed to stay professional. The Principal wasn't amused, she looked at the student with the sternest of looks, and said, "Excuse me son, but not only did you just yell out like someone with out any good sense, but you you used a word that has oppression attached to it. You need to see me later." A hush went over the class as the laughter that filled the air tuned melted into a stunned silence. At that moment, another student raised her hand, and when called on, asked "So, where you from?" "I'm actually from around here? I grew up right up the street." I replied point north. A few of the students looked really impressed, while some sat with their faces coated with pessimism. I continued to scan the room, and noticed that the diversity seen in the GREEN room, was absent from the RED room. The GREEN classroom was mixed, a seeming microcosm of America. Meanwhile, the RED room looked like that classrooms I grew up apart of, all Black and Hispanic. The bell rung and students darted from the classroom, like a sprinter when they hear the gun go off at the beginning of a race. The Principal turned to me and said as students had completely abandoned the class, "You ready? These are your kids now." I nodded solemnly, believing in my heart that I could do it. As I gazed upon the empty seats, I had the strongest blend of emotions, a sense of peace and an anxiety, somehow at the same time.

▼

Chapter 5

"Colors Pt. 2"

· · · · · · ·

After school ended, I stayed a bit longer to begin lesson planning for Monday. I didn't realize how much time and creativity it took to generate something for a group of 8th graders a do for about an hour a day. Well, I felt as if I was here, I was supposed to be here, so I worked. My brother called me at about 4:30 to see where I was, as he wanted to hang out with some old friends from our neighborhood. "Yo, when you leave school, I'll be outside. Matter fact, come out now." He urged. "I'm trying to get ready for Monday little bro." I responded. "You have Saturday and Sundar for that. Give yourself a break. Let's celebrate! I got the gang from way back meeting me at that new restaurant on 8th. They all wanted to see you." I thought about it for a second, and realized that I could have some fun and it would be great seeing a bunch of the old guys. "Alright, where you at? I'm on the way down now." I replied gleefully. "Outside already, I knew you'd say that." He said.

I packed my things, and flew out of the building to meet my brother who was sitting in the parking lot blasting music. The closer I got to him, I could hear the song that was playing, it was "Inner City Blues" by Marvin Gaye. I stepped into his truck and asked, "What you know 'bout this youngblood?" "Man, this a banger!" He replied. We drove out of the parking lot and up to the new diner on 8th, it was called "The Diamond Diner." Once we arrived, we immediately saw our old friends seated at a table. I ran up on them jumped on one of them and they all patted me on the back. I felt at home, dog piled on a bunch of dudes that once did the same with in football pads. Amongst people that I felt were my own. I'd realized it was the first time in a while that the company I was in were people who wanted nothing from me, except for my company. We sat down, as the waitress approached us to begin taking our orders. She was a thin black woman, with nose ring, sporting a natural hair style. "How can I help you gentlemen?" She asked politely. "Well first, I'll start by asking for an order of fries for the table and your number on the back of the bill, because I'll be paying." One of my friends said. "Chill bro..." My brother Cecil stated as we all laughed. "That's flattering sir, but what would you like?" She replied laughingly as well. We each went around giving our orders to her. "Thanks gentlemen, hope the food is good, and no you (pointing) cannot have my number." We all laughed as she continued, "there's a beer garden outside if you guys are interested, and I won't charge you additionally for it, since your friend's pick up line was so smooth." She left, and we each looked around at each other puzzled. One of our friends finally broke the ice by saying, "What the heck is a beer garden?" We each went outside, curious as to what this was exactly, and saw a host of people standing around drinking. My brother went to drink and mingle, but I just went back to the table with one of our friends. We sat down and the french fries came and just began talking. "Did you peep?" He said to me with a smirk on his face. "Yeah... but just so we are clear, what you talking about?" I replied. "Umm... there's a beer garden in the middle of our old hood. The only black people that drink beer are OG's. And it surely isn't as organized as this. Do you see what has happened." I shook my head as I dipped a French fry into the ketchup carton. What I had been seeing when I moved back was beginning to manifest before my eyes. I didn't say anything though, I just tried to have a good time.

After we had eaten, my brother and two of the three guys that were with us, had gotten a bit drunk. This drunkenness led to us being serenaded all the way back to the car. I had taken the keys, so we could avoid an accident and summoned my brother to hop into the car. "Yo, we took the train down here. You got us for a ride? Plus, I ain't bout to be on the train with these dudes." He said with a blend of concern and sarcasm. I agreed to take them and the five of us hopped in the car. I realized that I had left my drivers license at home, because I hadn't driven in quite a while, so I headed back to our house to grab it with the guys packed in the car like sardines. I slid into the house, grabbed my license, which was in what we called the "junk drawer" and headed back out the door. I left the car parked in the middle of the street, with hazards on, as there was not a car in sight behind us, and I was headed right back. I jumped back into the car and slowly pulled off taking my time as I was uneasy driving a truck, smoothly hitting a turn at the intersection of my block. Immediately, my brother looked out the rear view mirror and said half tired, "Cops, behind you..." This had to be a mistake. I mean, I legit didn't do anything, and it's highly unlikely that they saw me sitting in the middle of the block. I pulled over just as they put their sirens on. I wasn't nervous; I was in my neighborhood, I wasn't speeding, I have a license and everyone that had been drinking was over 21. Once the cop had officially stopped, and got out of the car I had put everything out onto the dashboard to prevent any unnecessary movement. He approached the driver's side with his partner on the passenger's side shining a flashlight into my brother's bloodshot, tired eyes. Two of the guys in the back were asleep, as the sober one decided to stay awake, but he stayed pretty quiet. "License and registration." He said firmly, while sucking on a lollipop. I said nothing, I simply pointed to the dashboard, grabbing the documents and handing them to him wearing the most uncomfortable of smiles. He looked at me a bit unamused, as if he was looking for something in particular. His partner, on the passenger side was scoping the car out with his flashlight. He went to the back of the car, as we all stared, after noticing the two asleep. "You fellas been drinking?" The cop next to me said stoically. "I haven't, sir, which is why I'm behind the wheel." I said calmly. He stared at me quietly, with the coldest of stares and then stretched his head to look in the back at our friends. "Are there any weapons in the car?" The second cops asked. "No, there aren't any weapons in the car. There are no drugs in here either, just in case you wanted to know. Because I'm sure it was going there." My brother said rolling his eyes. The second cop, noticing my brothers sarcasm, asked "Are you fellas from a round here?" "Yes, actually." I replied. "We grew up in this area, and have been living around the corner for pretty much all of our lives." "Hmmm..." The second cop said. "Well this ain't quite the neighborhood you grew up in anymore. And we like it that way, so let's make sure it remains that way." The first cop smiled, flung documents back into my lap and walked away. "This is not OUR neighborhood anymore." My friend shouted from the back.

▼

Chapter 6

"Lemons"

• • • • • • •

The incident stuck with me for the entire weekend. But, I didn't have much time to hold on to it, as the weekend seemingly flew and before I knew it, Monday was here. I was nervous. About to begin a journey I'd have never imagined. About to do something that one year ago was laughable to me. About to begin the journey as a shaper of the future.. in a place where it started for me. I arrived about an hour early to take it all in. As I stood around my classroom at all the empty desks, I got that feeling. That same feeling that I'd had when I stepped into my first college class. I remember arriving early to get a seat and just absorbing the magnitude of the moment for me. I didn't have a black teacher until I was in high school and here I was... a black male teacher. I made sure to double, triple and quadruple check my plans, as we were going to read Frederick Douglass. Before I knew it, the bell rang and waves of students could be heard filling the hallways. I stood at the door to greet them, as teachers were advised to do, and made sure that I was prepared to shake each hand, and greet each by name.

That was the plan.

The first student walks up to me and completely ignores me in exchange for her cell phone. as I extend my hand, smile, and ask her name. Two male students then approach, "Hi I'm your new teacher, Mr...." But before I could even finish, "Okay... okay..." Then amongst themselves, "yeah.. we ain't gonna see this boul too much longer..."

Students: 3

Teacher: 0

I didn't say a word to any other students that had walked by, I just smiled and nodded my head. I figured, once class started, I'd regroup.

After the final student walked in, I took a deep breath and headed to the front of the room. "Okay Red group." I shouted over the noise. "Take your books out, so you can start reading." I added. Nobody stopped talking. The volume, in fact, increased as I stood before a chaotic frozen in the moment. "Hey, sir..." A young lady said in a small voice that snuck through the noise. "You can ring that bell on the desk. It's the attention bell, a lot of teachers here use it so we kinda used to it." She added. I smiled with very little confidence, picked up the bell and rang it tenaciously, which made the noise quell to the point of silence. I looked at the young lady, smiled with confidence this time and began again. "Okay, take out your Frederick Douglass books. So you can do some reading..." "Could we read together, sir?" One kid shouted out, interrupting me. "Imma prolly fall asleep if we don't." I thought for a minute, "The kids are supposed to read silently to themselves." I looked around and saw that many kids were checking out as I took time to think about it."

"Sure!"

I didn't really care, and as long as they would stay quiet, I felt I'd be okay.

"Who would like to read?" I polled the class. Two students put their hands up, while the rest looked away. I wanted to get everyone involved, so I called in a random person. "You, young lady." I'd like for you read for us." I said with a smile. She stared back at me and said not a word. It was like a Wild West stare down, only missing the classic tumbleweed flying by. I waited a few seconds, before she finally nodded her head no. I didn't know her, but thought I would at least try to motivate her. "Come on.. why not?" I added. She continued to look at me with a blank stare, before nodding no again, and finally putting her head down. I understand the verbal cues, so I moved on to another child. "Hey, young man... can you do it?" I asked another student. At this statement, the class collectively dropped their heads and some even began to snicker. I caught the hint, and simply called on one of the students that had their hand up. I jumped between the two watching the rest of the class. Some following along, some looking out the window, while some attempted to follow along, but not even looking at the right page. We read together until the class ended. When the bell rang, students cleared the class out and made a beeline for the phone. I dialed the Principal's, where she picked up after one ring. I told her I had a question and if she could meet me for a few minutes a I had the next two periods off. When she agreed, I hung up the phone and sprinted down to her office. When I got to the main office, the door to the principal's office was already open. I walked in to see her seated behind her desk which contained a mountainous pile of papers beside her computer, which she was typing diligently on. She stopped and looked at me saying, "Hey, how can I help you?" I felt bad for a moment because she seemed really busy, but I persisted. "Yeah... so, my first class wasn't bad, but I noticed only two kids were willing to read. Some kids who were chaotic at the beginning of the class, literally did talk for the rest of the period. I figured that because they seemed talkative at the beginning, I could use that to my advantage. She looked at me as if there was something she hadn't told me.. as if there was something I needed to know.

"Well, the Red groups are the groups that represent our students who are behind. What happens in other schools is, they put them special education, saying there's something wrong, when they are simply behind. I don't like that mode of thinking, I believe our students are not failures, they have been failed. Failed by these schools that have merely treated them like a number. So, I didn't want them to walk around being labeled... Black children deal with that enough. Which is why I'm buried in all of this paperwork, to make sure our kids get the services and their needs are met. So, be creative, find ways to push them to read. First, you may want to get to their confidence in you as the teacher."

I totally understood. I was them, at one time seated in the exact same seats.

▼

Chapter 7

"Lemonade"

· · · · · · ·

That night, my brother and our friends sat outside on the steps and talked. It was one of those cool, crispy fall evenings, so we were all wearing hoodies. I always hated that one of my friends used to always put his hoodie on and pull the drawstrings so tight that he looked like child about to exit the womb. "This that style homie! You don't know nothin' bout this..." Just as he finished, the faint reflection of red and blue sirens grew more and more definitive against the walls of the newly constructed homes. It was the police, specifically the same police officers who pulled us over a few days prior. "They pulled up slowly, getting out of the car with their hands shadowing their guns as if they were waiting for one of us to pull out a weapon. "Can I help you officer?" I said before any of my friends could speak. "No, actually." He replied somewhat squinting his eyes. "Well, why are approaching us, if I may ask." My brother blurted rather quizzically. "We just wanted to see what was what? We heard that there was a shooting not too far away and considering there aren't too many of you left here, we wanted to make sure that you guys weren't involved." The second cop said. The four of us looked at each other while the two officers stood amongst us, waiting for us to start talking again. None of said a word, we just stared at each other and them. This awkward silence was broken once one of the officers said, "Have a good evening gentlemen...and be careful with those hoodies." They walked away slowly, got into their cars with arrogant smiles across both of their faces. They nodded at us, laughed and sped off as we each hung our heads in utter confusion and disgust.

The next day, I went to work totally not in the mood; the police interaction, and on top of that I had to deal with the kids. I sat at my desk just before the school day started, completely exasperated with a cup of coffee that wasn't making life any better. The children came in as rambunctious as usual, with seemingly no regard for me, as I miserable attempted to welcome them into the room. The bell rang and I closed the door with my the sounds of varied conversations filling the room. I walked to the front and began trying to "shush" the crowd, but the effort went to no avail. I locked eyes with a young lady whose hands were folded and seemingly prepared to learn. She looked and me, then cut her eyes to the bell. I quickly remembered the bell from the previous day, grabbed it and began to ring. The conversations quelled to the point that I could only hear one conversation going on and it was between that student who everyone hung their heads at the day before and the young man behind them. "He sucks, I'm wayyy better than he is... wait til gym class. I'm killin bul... It ain't gonna be enough tape to help his ankles for when he catch this crossover..." The first student said, while completely turned around. "Excuse me, fellas you are holding the class up, we need to get it started." I yelled over the class. The second student got quiet and sat back in his chair, while the first tried to continue the conversation. I walked to the back of the room to address him, as each student seemingly watched in horror, "What's going on? I need you to stop talking so we can learn." He turned his head and looked at me with a squinted face, "Old head... go head somewhere. Ain't nobody tryna get on your wave. We chillin over here." "No sir, you are. Your friend over here is in position to learn, he's tryna get his." I replied. "Aight, well whatever... this don't mean nothin to me anyway." He replied with an attitude. "And why is that?" I asked. "Because, at the end of the day no one of us are going anywhere. You know how many niggas I see on the way here that tell me they went to this school? You knows up with that statement in the first place? The fact that I see them on the way here. Like, why ain't you at work dog? Why ain't you doin nothing with ya life? They all come from here. The lucky ones get out this hole, but the rest of us get left here to be nobody's basically. We gotta rap, or play ball because we don't have money or whatever else we need to do anything else. And if you look around, thats all we see niggas ain't in school because they one the courts and on the corners. Doin what we was destined to do. It's a cycle, and we see it and we be it."

I couldn't respond. I just stared at him and walked back to the front of the class.

Just as I headed back to the front the chatter began yet again. Just before it could get rambunctious I yelled in emotional anguish, "Please, be quiet people!" Every voice stopped instantly, and students sat up in their seats. I exhaled deeply and instantly regretted yelling. I was taking my frustrations out on kids, and felt the need to apologize. Just as I went to do so, a voice from the right side said, "are you okay?" I looked out on to a sea of confused and somewhat concerned faces and said, "This is tough, and I've only been here one day. Plus, on top of that, the cops rolled up on me and some friends for no real reason last night. They've been acting funny since I moved back around here."

At that moment, a young lady's hand slipped into the air.

"My brother said the same thing has been happening to him too. He said he was coming home from work and he works late nights cleaning trains. He had his hood on and his boots so I guess they thought he looked sketchy. Anyway, he walked off the bus and didn't even get a block before a cop car was right next to him. They started asking him questions and even tried to get out and check him. My brother was confused because he's like, 'I'm from round here...what is y'all doin?' My mom said it was something called over policing. Sh said cause' the white people start getting houses on our block, the cops started trippin'."

After she finished another student raised his hand, and shared an encounter.

"Me one of my guys, and my homegirl were outside... on my homegirl's porch, mind you. We were just chillin and a squad car pulled up right behind her dads van. We ain't think nothing of it, because we kind of used to seein cops, this where it gets crazy. The two cops quietly walked out of the car, and out of nowhere gripped my friend up, pinned him to my homegirl's van chest first and stuck a gun in his lower back. Me and my homegirl were like 'what are y'all doing?' Cop gave no explanation, just told us with a smile to 'calm down.' My homegirl's mom came out and said, 'excuse me officer?' I don't know what happened after that because they told me to go in the house."

He shrugged his shoulders as he stopped speaking. At that moment, another hand went up to the point that we had spent the entire class sharing experiences with each listening in respectfully and agreeing with the other. The bell rang and the kids instantly turned the the classroom into a ghost town, however the young man who I had had the encounter with stayed behind. I took my time, pretending to clean up non existent trash and straighten books that were barely crooked before I got to him. "Hey, you good?" I said solemnly. "Yeah, I'm aight. I just want to apologize. You seem like a cool old head and I don't want no smoke." He said in a low tone with his eyes fixated on his hands, which were tapping rhythmically on the desk. "I appreciate that you shared that with us, because I see the same thing when I go home. Cops always looking, and I hate the they takin the hood away. Wish it was something I could do about it.... Anyway, I need to go to lunch... I'll see you tomorrow." He said as he grabbed his backpack and sprinted out of the classroom.

▼

Chapter 8

"Juice"

• • • • • • •

After the school that day, we sat in the conference room for what is called "Professional Development" which seemed to only develop my boredom into insanity, but my attention was grabbed when they began speaking about students. The counselor, Mrs. Fox, was leading the PD in which she'd highlight certain students to give teachers reports on their behavior and backgrounds. I felt I'd use it as an opportunity to learn about some of the students in my class to better work with them.

"Okay, so here's our first student, he's apparently a member of one of his neighborhood gangs, and they are currently at war with another from the area. Many of the students who are apart of these rival gangs attend this school, so we have constant threats of friction between the two. He also tests behind reading and math levels, so we have to monitor that we are properly handling his case. We haven't left him back because... of... legalities, but it's been a struggle for teachers to get through to him. He doesn't speak... almost at all, so we wonder if we should give him speech classes. We just try to make sure that he's here, because he comes late everyday, so it's a win that we get that. So, please monitor him if you can."

She continued to go through students, but I was too fixated on the first one she spoke on. He didn't speak much, but he said something to me. I also noticed that he spoke fluently to me, but used a great deal of slang with his friends. I had a plan, and execution of this plan was imminent.

The next morning, I had arrived early... again to prepare myself for what was preparing for me. I simply took the precious day as an anomaly and was ready for combat; I was prepared to yell if I needed to, and throw kids out, etc. I stood at the window watching the magenta sky finally feeling somewhat confident about what I was about to embark upon, when suddenly an announcement goes over the loud speaker. I wasn't sure if this was normal, but the again I was new. The serenity that accompanied beautiful scenery that overlooked the city, quickly shifted to a panic as a distressed voice said over the loud speaker, "please excuse the interruption, we need all teachers and staff outside on the yard... a large fight has ensued!" I didn't even grab my jacket, before I darted out of the classroom like a torpedo, flying through the hallway, then down the stairs and out to the yard. There was a big crowd and it was tough to tell who was fighting and who was standing around spectating. Just I ran out a few other teachers emerged from the doors and we started grabbing grabbing students and pulling them apart. From the onset we noticed that many of the kids didn't even attend our school, and I believe that our office staff knew that as she called the police from her office. As we plowed through the mass of kids swinging over us and kicking people who were down, the police showed up. They proceeded to do the same, but with seeming ruthless intent. One officer even put his hand near his pocket to draw his weapon, it another grabbed him by the hand, firmly advising him not to. The chaotic scene eventually died down as we had all of the students who were fighting contained. The officers, however grabbed the kids who were not from our school, pinned them to the ground aggressively and had them handcuffed. They sat with their knees planted firmly in the small of their backs as they mirandized them. I scanned the yard only to notice the kid being held tightly by his ripped jacket by another teacher. He had a minor scratch on his face which was the source of a small amount of blood that had been smeared upon his uniform shirt by the scuffling. He hurled curse words at rival members and even attempted to break free and kick one of them while the cops were taking them away. One of the Non-Teaching Assistants got word from the principle through their walkie talkie that they wanted all of our students back in the building and brought into the main office. We each held tightly to our students to ensure that they wouldn't break free, as we escorted them into the office. The 7 AM sun was still beaming across the tops of computers and chairs when we brought our students into the main conference room. There were too many of them to house in the main office's lobby area, so we had to hold them in the conference room. "Hey, can a few of you guys stay behind stay back and sit with these young men while I talk to the police?" The principle asked in a tone that suggested that she wasn't actually asking. Each of the three of us looked at each other, shrugging our shoulders.

When the principal left, one of the teachers, Mr. Brown, attempted to break the ice by saying, "So what's going on? Why did you guys fight? You know that..." At that moment, he paused, scanning the room realizing that none of the 7 students were paying attention to him. He cleared his throat to get their attention, and recover his pride, "So, nobody is going to talk?" The students were either looking at the floor or each other with dead serious stares as the second teacher, Mr. Black picked up, "You busy are just wrong for that. We're here trying to help you and you ignore us? You guys are better than that." He continue to lecture them as they stared away from him with faces of both anger and sadness. "Well fine. We are still here, and we do care... we just want to see if we could help." Mr. Black finished. He and Mr. Brown left the room out frustration, and I felt them. I could relate with trying to help and being denied in some way. Just as the door closed, my student said in a dark, monotone, "See, y'all niggas be out here on some nut stuff. Y'all don't seem to get that we ain't letting' our set go out like that. You heard about a shooting from the other night? That was one of our guys. We told the, niggas that as soon as we see em, it's on sight out here. Forget whatcha heard. And I hope I see em again to give em' more work." After speaking, he sat quietly, just as the other boys did, looking seemingly through the office wall positioned ahead of him. I curiously tilted my head forward slightly, anticipating that he and the other boys may have said something else. I couldn't understand why they chose to talk to me, who said nothing to them, and totally ignored the other two teachers who were in the room. "Don't say nothing tho, old head..." Another one said to me. I didn't respond, nor did I have time to as the Principal had come back in the talk to the boys. "You're good now. You should head up, your students are on the way to your classroom." She said to me as she walked in. I nodded, and took one last glance at the room, and all the boys faces, collectively showed content. I didn't get it, and did t have time to either.

My kids were standing outside of my classroom as I approached the door. They were talkative, per usual, as I let them into the room where they'd drop their bags and get seated. I was prepared for war, even more so at this point, as I felt that my first few days had been a bit of proving ground for me. I stepped to the front of the class and before I could say a word, or pick up the bell, students seemed to have quieted on their own. I was confused; it had already been an auspicious day, and now it got flat out strange. "Is everybody good? I mean, Im not upset, but y'all okay?" I asked the class with a timid smile. A laughter went over the room, when one young man said, "You aiight with us old head. We respect you. I mean, you just keep coming back and you ain't all in ya feelings. We like you, and I feel like you relate." The rest of the class shook their heads in agreement as one young lady said, "Yeah... like my dad be sayin from old movie he like, your got da juice now.'"

▼

Chapter 9

"The Outside In" Pt 2

· · · · · · ·

"He's a black man. The rest of y'all just wouldn't understand." This was said by my student who had been involved in the fight after his conference with the Principal and the counselor, Mrs. Fox. He was indeed suspended for his actions and had to stay out of school for a week. "The school district passed that down." The Principal said once we got to speak at the end of the school day. "I just don't understand how you can expect a kid to be a better member of society, if you're going to punish them by removing them from the safest, most productive environment. I'm not saying that the fighting should go unpunished, but what if he decides to fight out of school? That fight was with people from his neighborhood, so what if they just... fight in the neighborhood? What if it's worse and there's no one to step in. What if it goes too far? I just don't get this whole punitive thing, especially because there's no restoration attached to it. He did say that he wanted you to do his home visits...if you're comfortable with it. He trusts you for some reason. I find that interesting because he's never really attached himself to anybody other than the kids from his neighborhood that go here and before we could even speak on it, he said, 'Can he do my home visit?' I don't mess with the rest of y'all. Plus, he's a black man.' Mrs Fox asked him why was that so significant, he straight told her, your wouldn't understand.' I guess we haven't had many black teachers, so some of the young men kind of look to you. So, hear, take this work... his address is listed on the top sheet, make sure you get to him at some point this week. Thank you."

It wasn't until I had left the school that I realized that she hadn't actually given me a choice.

On my way home, I decided I'd just go right then and there; he didn't live too far away, and I honestly just wanted to get it over with. I walked for about 10 minutes before I had gotten to his block which was desolate and deserted. There was very little evidence of humanity other than the cars that sat in front of the five homes on the block. Aside from that, there were a host of cranes and material designed to build homes. There were about 15 homes being erected, with what was apparently new renovation. I peeked into one of the homes to see recessed lighting being input, and in one, which had the entire first floor completed, I was able to see into the kitchen area which had brand new stainless steel appliances. After snooping for a few minutes I knocked on his door and was greeted by a little girl holding a doll as if it was her child. "Hi, who are you?" She said from behind a screen door with the sweetest voice. "Hi, I'm here for your brother, I'm his teacher. I came by to bring him his work." I responded. "Hold on..." She replied as she closed the door. I could hear her over the sound of drills and cranes moving, speaking to what sounded like an authority figure. The door opened and a woman answered saying, "Hi! Come on in. I know it's a little chilly outside." "Thank you..." I replied as I entered the home. When I walked in, I saw plastic on all of the furniture, which I knew meant that I needed to ask before I sat down. I didn't know how to approach the, so I just stood. As I stood waiting, an older woman was slowly making her way down the stairs. "Sit down baby... we about to have dinner, I can fix you a plate. If you want." She said. "Oh, I'm quite alright ma'am. Thanks though!" I responded. Just behind her, my student came down, he was wearing a red football jersey with the number 7 on it, with basketball sweat pants and socks on. He gave me a head nod to which I nodded back. "Can we sit outside and rap?" He asked. "Sure." I replied subtly. He opened the door before me, and led me out the door. We sat on the steps in silence, both just looking around. The air, filled with dust from the gravel produced by the work being done. At one point, he fixed his eyes on one of the newly constructed houses. "They're killing the hood, man. It's not fair." He said. He then pointed at an empty lot where a port-a-potty sat, "That used to be filled with kids. Me and my friends used to kick it over there, jump on old mattresses, play ball, and all that. I used to kill them too! Now, they got these white dudes that ain't even from here, showing tryna bring in all of these white families, man. All my friends are gone too. It's only a few houses on this block anyway. Us, a few old people and one of my friends. My grandmom own our house and she said that when she die, she gonna pass it to my my, then to me and my sister. She straight told us, 'Do not sell this house! This a family house!' For like months some dude in a suit with this curly hair and a weird accent, like he from like Boston or something, say he'd like to buy the house. He came to me and my grandma all polite, gave my sister candy, and even tried to hit on my mom, tryna get in. I see him almost everyday, so I think he's directing these dudes that's doing the work. It's wack though. They taking my hood...my home."

I felt his pain.

I wanted to go home, because I was starting to get cold, but I sensed that he may not have wanted me to go. "They're doing the same thing in my neighborhood. I left for a little while because I was working for the Mayor, and when I came back, my neighborhood started to look like this. There were families missing, and all that." I said to him wearing at the half demolished abandoned home. "I want to do something, but I don't know what to do. I want my home back...." Cutting him off, I said, "I noticed that when you talk to me, you speak with very little slang, but when you're around your others, including the other adults, you switch it up. What's up with that? You know that the Principal and the Counselor, Mrs. Fox believes that you have issues with speech? I don't think there's any wrong, and I certainly don't think you're behind in anything." I said sternly. He exhaled and said, "First off, the gang doesn't care about that smart guy stuff. They say 'you talk white,' when you speak with proper English. When they added that restaurant a few blocks from here, I thought that was cool, it was different, but the gang was like, 'nah we ain't eating there. They make that white people stuff!' They look at the menu and be like, 'Whats that!' And make fun of it. But, what's crazy is that the white people be doing the same thing. I see them walking by here, when they look at the houses, how the teachers approach us, they look at us as inferior, like we asked for the hood to be the way it is or something. They equate it with black, because they don't treat the white kids the same way. It's funny, because it's like black people and white people be seeing things in black and white… like aspects of society don't blend or something/can't blend or something… anyways, let me get my work cause it's time for dinner. Thanks old head, I'll see you in like a week." He grabbed the folder from my hands and started for the door. "Hey…" I said. If you got a problem with them taking the hood, let's do something. I got your back. In a week, when you're back at school. I expect you to have come up with something to do." He slightly bobbed his head back as if I was crazy, and replied, "I'm 13, what am I supposed to do." I smiled as I turned away saying, "Figure it out…" I walked away and could hear him faintly saying, "Aight old head, you need to figure out a barber though…"

▼

Chapter 10

"The Inside Out" PT. 2

· · · · · · ·

A week had gone by, and I honestly had forgotten about the deal that I had made with my student. The class was getting better; I mean I was terrible at teaching, the kids had a bit of respect for me so I guess I was okay. They were understanding too, some telling me, "hey, just be confident, you're doing okay... we like having you as our teacher!"

I guess.

Exactly one week after I sat with my student on his steps, he returned to school. It was early, in fact it was just before school had begun so I was getting the classroom set up. I was at the board, about to write out objectives, when I heard a knock on the glass window that sat in the middle of the wooden door. I turned only to see the top of a head with a dark caesar haircut, sporting thick waves. I walked to the door, wondering why any student would voluntarily be at school this early and he walked in without saying a word to me. The silence that filled the air was broken by the jingling sound of steel zippers moving about as he moved. He sat down at his desk, and took a book out. Before I could get a word out, "Check this out." He said pointing to the book. I said nothing, as he had and simply picked up the book. He had a plan. A plan headed with a title reading, "Put the Hood Back in Neighborhood." He had a page long, elaborate plan for a rally in the neighborhood to better the area.

"So, what's your logic? I thought your problem was with all the work being done in your neighborhood?" I asked.

"Yeah, but I thought about it a bit and for real for real, we could use the work. It, I want neighborhood improvement. If y'all gonna put this money, and of the city is gonna let people just buy land, they should consult with the people first. The ones that live here already. Make sure we good first. Make sure we are okay before you just pass off land. Ask us what we need and how they can be a service to us. If you gonna come in, cool, just don't let it be at the downfall of people who live here already."

I was honestly impressed.

"I'm not sure how far this is going to go, because people can buy what they want, but letting the city know that you want better for your neighborhood is doable." I said somewhat nervously. "I want to do it with the school though, they'll listen to y'all if y'all do it. I'm just some young bul from around the way. Could you give this to the Principal for me?" He asked sincerely. I agreed and he put his books away going into the hallway to wait for his friends. I emailed the Principal asking to meet with her that day; I wanted to continue to earn his trust, so I had to make sure I followed through. Once school had begun students came rambunctiously into class and most seemed to have really miss our suspended student. Kids seemed to swarm his desk, and I honestly did mind, I'm sure he appreciated that support and maybe he needed it. We started class and I made the announcement about his rally and I gave him the opportunity to tell the class what he told me. Many of the students looked at each other, surprised that I'd ask him to say anything publicly in class. Their sense of surprise morphed into shock when he actually spoke. He commanded their attention with his poignance, and clarity. As he spoke, the Principal walked into the class with her eyebrows raised. she gestured to me to come to the back of the room. I walked to the back to meet her, where she seemed focused on the room. "Good stuff." She said with a face of affirmation. "Thanks, but this isn't the lesson..." I replied with a whisper. "Doesn't matter, this is still good stuff. You've got kids in here talking, especially our man here. I'm pleased." She said pointing to the front of the classroom. I got an email alert from my phone while I was was walking down the hallway, and saw that you wanted to talk. It looks like your class is sustaining itself at this point, can we talk right here?" I looked around a bit and saw that at this point students were really engaged to the point of asking questions. So, I started, "He wants to do a rally, against the mishandling of his neighborhood, over policing, and all that. He wanted me to talk to you. I'm not all that sure about it, I feel like it may be a little under developed, but I do feel we should empower this young man." I said to her. "I actually think that we should push our kids to do more. So much of what we do inside the walls of these schools gets lost somewhere in the process of them leaving the building. I feel that need to be DOING something. That's what I believe is missing in the educational process. So, let's get behind him. Did he say when he wanted to do it?" She replied. "Not that I recollect. But you can ask him when he wants to do it." Just as I finished my thought the white noise that sat in the background, erupted into what appeared to be a full on protest. Students forcefully got up from their desks. A few students pulled out their cellphones streaming the raucous on social media, as the Principal and I stood still. I went to say something, but as I moved, the Principal, who stood with her eyes laser focused on what was happening in front of her, grabbed my hand sternly as if to tell me not to move.

The raucous apparently spread quickly as students from other classes began walking out of their classrooms to come to ours. Before long, the Principal and I stood above an ocean of 6th, 7th and 8th graders who were all collectively chanting, "SAVE OUR HOODS! SAVE OUR HOODS!" Students began moving out of the classrooms through the hallways, chanting loudly as teachers watched in dismay. I stood beside the Principal as she wore a look of satisfaction, while the students marched through the hallways, led by a student who just days before was seemingly cast aside. By the time students had gone outside, the teachers and staff had begun following behind them. Some teachers were a bit offended that students had simply walked out of their rooms in the middle of instruction. One teacher in particular, Mr. Martin, could be heard saying behind us, "These kids.. unruly. You try to teach them and this is how they respond. They don't care anything about science, but the second something crazy happens, they are all over it. This is why they are where they are..." The Principal stopped at that moment, turning around slowly, and I could tell that Mr. Martin didn't think that anyone had heard him. *"These kids?* I'm sorry, but if you can't see *our kids* as *your kids...* if you can't take ownership over the young people you stand before, than you don't need to be here. Good luck in your future endeavors..." She said this and kept walking. He stood there, flustered as the crowd proceeded forward. While Mr. Martin represented the thoughts of some, there were others who took a different perspective. Mr. Black waxed poetic about the move. "This is so wonderful, to see the power of our black and brown students through activities like these just pushes me further to teach. I absolutely love this work... working with our students of color... and this just makes it all worth it."

Mr. Black was happy, needless to say.

We got outside to what appeared to be the entire student body standing on the school yard. Kids had taken cardboard sheets from the art room, and written signs that said, "Save our hoods..." and "Construct some other place..." It was a sight indeed, so much so, that people from the neighborhood had grown curious. Looking across the street at the residents from the neighborhood, I saw the older residents cheering the young on. Many came to their doors in support of the young people's' boldness to stand for what they felt passionately about.

I saw Mr. and Mrs. Cleaver walking up with smiles across their faces. They came over to me, each putting their arms around me. Mr. Cleaver gazed upon the mass of children Smiling from ear to ear proclaiming, "This is what we needed. Young people... instead of engaging in violence, engaging in activism. This is what we created this community center for. This is why we stuck around. This, is what your mother died for." I knew my mom's story, her plight, why she died and that she was killed during a protest, and that's why I always cared about the community, no matter how I approached it, I always tried to have people in mind. "Yeah..." I replied with a sigh. "Not sure if you had anything to do with this, but I feel like you did. School ain't never have nothing like this, until you came through. Principal likes too, maybe in more ways than one." Mrs. Cleaver said as we looked at the organized chaos created by our youth. "We don't exist if our youth aren't doing anything. Generations die...voices get lost when young people are pacified." She added. My brother walked up at that moment, with his work uniform on. "Hey, I was on one of my rounds and I had radio on, when they said there was a riot going on and telling people to avoid the area. They said that the kids might have been dangerous. I heard it was the elementary school and was like 'no way!' Had to come check this out for myself. I see it's just more of that nonsense media portrayal."

The police pulled up in droves and I saw this going south.

The cops frantically got out of their cars and ran into the crowds of middle schoolers. Many students stood their grounds as police hurled obscenities blended into orders to move back into the building. Cops continued to move in, ultimately going to the residents at their doors, screaming at them to go into the house. Many of the residents stayed, shouting back that they were within their rights to stand on their properties, which in turn mattered not to the cops. The four of us were greeted by two officers who had tasers drawn, forcefully yelling, "Get back!" At this point, we didn't really feel threatened, because we weren't actually doing anything." Aww you poor babies, y'all feel so threatened by us, and we aren't even doing anything! Mrs. Cleaver said. "That's America for you, I guess." She added. "Y'all stay coming in here thinking we doing something wrong... Y'all stay with your guns drawn. Yall been getting crazy lately. Out here trying to pull people over because you wanna please them very construction workers that the young out here protesting. Yall ain't bother to get to know who was here first... You ain't even peep that the people you are harassing, are the residents. Ain't your job to serve and protect? (Laughs) Serve and protect who? These new white folks that's moving down here? That's what I think it is. Y'all see our area as a cash cow, and y'all tryna pressure us to go, or force us to stay "in line," so it looks more pleasurable to them. Where was all this ten years ago. I didn't start seeing y'all until I started seeing them" My brother said sarcastically as he pointed to the developers. The first officer, who according to his badge was Officer Williams, looked very nervous, as he wasn't quite used to people who weren't immediately intimidated by him. Mr. Cleaver stepped forward, "We appreciate your presence, but this ain't y'all battle. This is between us and the people who feel the need to 'better' our neighborhoods. I like 'better', everybody should, but it's shouldn't be at the expense of people who have created legacies here. And for what? So y'all can experience a culture you find fascinating on TV? Only to find that the culture exists within the people... we make the experience, so when we go, it dies.

Or, are you just gonna uproot us because it's more 'convenient' to move into our areas? You save gas money by taking trains that were pissy, and terribly taken care of, only for you to come in and say the things we've been saying for decades... to which the city finally moves. Well guess what? As you can see, you won't discourage us out of our neighborhoods. We will fight you."

"That's it, you're under arrest." The second cop said. He signaled across the chaos to a few other officers who ran through the mass of protesting children to arrest the four of us. He grabbed us, slamming Mr. Cleaver to the ground, and planting his knee firmly in his back. "It won't look to good to the Mayor that the head of that little center is about to be arresting for threatening an officer. We yelled at him to release him, as we were being taken away. I glanced at the second officer's name plate, so I could at some point report the harassment and it read, "Lynch." The protest continued, as a few students who had been forcefully pushed back into the building stood watching what was happening. After seeing their colleagues' attention drawn to the arrests, they took focused on us. Some kids began taking their phones out to record the aggression by the police. I saw a cop pulling students to take their phones away from them, while teachers, white and black, yelled back at the cops' overpolicing. Who would've thought that something so peaceful, the brainchild of a student, would've veered in this direction. My brother were thrown into the cop car and all we could do was sit in the back of the car staring angrily at each other. We looked out of the window at the police shoving kids and teachers alike into the building, with their weapons drawn, awaiting someone to oblige them. I looked at my student, who was at the center of all of this and simply nodded my head in affirmation. I didn't want him to think that he was responsible, for what was happening to us.

Once the crowd was back under control, many parents had shown up, hearing that a "riot" had ensued at the school, but the police had it under control. Most took their kids out of school for the day. Some, didn't show up, which left kids in a school building with all types of emotions running rampant. The two officers had finally gotten into the car, but they're weren't officer Williams and Officer Lynch, one of them looked totally unfamiliar, while the other was an incredibly familiar face. It was the cop who had pulled us over, and walked up on us. My brother sighed heavily, and hung his head, while I sucked my teeth and twisted my lips. He looked back at us and said, "You two again... and you (Looks at me) the Mayor would be happy to know that you're out making mischief....again. You can't just go quietly, can you? You'll lose your little job soon and won't be able to do anything after a while."

Yet again.

When we got to the police station, the Mayor was awaiting me. They sat me down, handcuffed, at a desk in room away from my brother. The Mayor who was sitting, stood up, and began speaking, "Listen, you've got a lot in you. I've never refuted that, nor will I ever. But, you just don't get the game, do you? If you want to make it, you need to stay in *their* good graces. Yes, them (points out of the window at the officers) as well as *theeemmmm...* (He points out of the main window). You gotta get these white folks on your side. How do you think I was able to maintain being Mayor in this town? I honestly, only won because you destroyed the opposition in front of TV cameras, to which they couldn't deny me. I thought I could convey that you, bu I just couldn't, so to keep these people happy and myself in office because you're never too early to start thinking about re-election, I've got to make you disappear." He said, as he looked at me disappointedly. He got up and walked out of the room slamming the door behind him. A second later, my brother was tossed into the room by two officers who sat him down directly next to me. "Before we proceed here," he said, "What are your names?" Just as I began to speak, the officer interrupted saying, "It doesn't matter what their names are.... we can do that once we process them." He stood directly in front of us, leaned over and said, "You people don't deserve the neighborhoods you live in." At that moment the officer backhand smacked my brother, while another grabbed me from the chair and gripped me up against the wall. "You won't be starting any riots nor will you be disturbing the peace in OUR neighborhoods anymore."

Epilogue

To Whom May Concern,

I'm not dead. I honestly thought that I would be, but they spared my brother and I. Police brutality is a thing. They were successful in getting us out of the neighborhood, as the Mayor had the man who was renting to us, and had been since my mom was there, in his pocket. He essentially had some claim against us, allowing him to break the lease. The Mayor did, however, make a few calls to to the suburbs and got me a teaching job out there. He said, "You know too much for me to just move you out of the way and leave you there. You could take me to court and possibly win. So, I'll at least let you stay in education, since you seem to want to do that." I said, "whatever." I miss my students though. I wish I could go see them, they are just so cool. Plus, we were just getting to know each other. The Principal keeps me posted through email, as she always says to me, "the fight isn't over!" She says that they've been doing much better, scores are increasing and the "riot" as it was publicized actually brought some attention to the school. After that, they rallied at the School District building for better resources, funding and a host of other things, and because of this progressive reputation the school was getting, the school district had to bend. The protests actually reached the state level, which they saw as revolutionary. Our student, Amir, who led the charge has been doing well too. He texts me from time to time to check up on me. Last thing he said to me was, "they out here trippin'. We got all these crazy white people in our school now, looking in classrooms, wanting to interview me and stuff. I ain't wit it tho. I don't do all dat' talking. Like, why y'all in here now? What, y'all see our power and want to get a piece of it? Or, are y'all tryin to extinguish it or something? I don't know..." I always try to tell him that it's not all bad, and that it's cool to bring exposure to what you're doing. Hey, who knows, he may inspire someone else to do the same thing.

Mr. Cleaver was given won a case against the cop who beat on him. He's an older man, so his a bit more brittle than the rest of us. He used the money to upgrade the community center. Now, they have computers and all that stuff for kids to do all types of activities on. He also, used the money to expand the center to create jobs for people. Amir works with them in the summer, holding down the job I had when I first left, but in an apprentice sense.

My brother Cecil, is selling insurance and he's been very good at it, actually. He's able to help us afford the apartment we're living in, which is in the suburbs, so it's cool. We had to come up here because the Mayor's pull is limited out here. Nobody knows us, and we are so far out of peoples' way that I'm not even sure they realize we live here. I went down to the old neighborhood, just to drive through, and it's even more different than it was when we left. There's new housing, and needless to say the demographic has changed. It didn't feel the same as when I left it..and honestly, maybe that change was good. I don't know though, it's just something about you home not feeling like YOUR home.

My classroom is okay. I went from teaching a class of mostly all black kids to teaching kids who are all white, with about two black students. It's all good though, I'm making it. The relatability is different, so I'm figuring that part out. It's nice to be a black representation to people who don't typically see it, and surprising that students have responded really well to me. Many students are genuinely curious about where I come from, where I taught and how I grew up. They actually seem to really like me too. It's interesting because it seems like kids see the world in color as opposed to seeing things like adults seem to see them, in black and white. The parents, on the other hand consistently test my knowledge; it seems like they want me to fail, so that they can report me or something. The first day I walked in to my new classroom, I dropped my bag off at the table and emptied my materials and realized that a rock had come out. It was a stone that I'd received as a gift some time ago, and I actually forgot it was there. That rock was a reminder to me, a reminder that you have to start somewhere and sometimes you've got to start multiple times over.

Printed in the United States
By Bookmasters